JUSTICE

Alden, Thanks.

JUSTICE

by
Jay Lillie

Ivy House Publishing Group
www.ivyhousebooks.com

PUBLISHED BY IVY HOUSE PUBLISHING GROUP
5122 Bur Oak Circle, Raleigh, NC 27612
United States of America
919.782.0281
www.ivyhousebooks.com

ISBN: 978-1-57197-506-5

Library of Congress Control Number: 2010942138

© 2010 Jay Lillie

Printed in The United States of America

DEDICATED TO

Madeleine and Jim

Who together launched me with love and the freedom to succeed or fail.

TABLE OF CONTENTS

ACKNOWLEDGEMENTS

The author acknowledges the support and friendship of *The Honorable ROBINSON O. EVERETT, judge, distinguished lawyer, defender of our freedoms, and Duke Law School professor*, who from the moment we first met until the day he left this world gave me his friendship and unrelenting encouragement to pursue the crafting of this story.

Profound thanks to *LAURA TAYLOR*, a successful novelist in her own right, who has extricated me from a lawyer's life of telling, and managed my progression into the novelist's art of showing.

THE UNITED STATES CONSTITUTION, and the Supreme Court *JUSTICES* and legal scholars who have their hands full keeping us free.

AUTHOR'S NOTE

The United States Constitution is a simple, straightforward document until it needs to be applied to living persons and everyday situations. Billions of hours and dollars have been spent over more than two centuries shaping its words and bending its intentions to meet certain ends. Its very simplicity has made it an exercise field for lawyers and Constitutional scholars.

The drafters used a minimum of well-chosen words, simply stated, to craft the Constitution into the spine of our nation. You can look at the document in two parts . . . the first is structural, setting up an Executive Branch to implement its terms and the terms of all laws passed by the Legislative Branch, and adding a Supreme Court to keep them both, and us, on the straight and narrow. The second part is the Bill of Rights, comprised originally by Amendments 1-10.

In the Bill of Rights, citizenship plays virtually no role.

In the structural segment, citizenship has an all-important function. In one form or another, the President and members of Congress are required to be citizens. However, nothing can be found in the words of the Constitution about citizenship being required to sit as a Justice on the United States Supreme Court.

Therein lies a tale . . .

CHICAGO

Six feet two inches tall, or you might say long since he'd been placed on his back in an alley with bare feet pointing into the night air, shadows of a dark beard on chalk white skin, blue eyes, jet-black wavy hair, arms folded across his chest, and necktie neatly knotted. The young man was as handsome as he was dead.

Detective Julia Gold of the Chicago police department turned away from the body on the slab, setting her jaw and shaking her right hand like she'd just burned it on a hot stove.

One of the lab technicians nearby smiled. "He probably died face down, or the reaction can be caused by blood rushing there during a forceful smothering. That scratch on his nose might indicate he fell down face first, but we'll check for other signs that he was smothered."

Julia raised her eyebrows and nodded. "Thanks for the anatomy lesson, Sue. I'll be around if you find a clue on what this hunk might have been doing back in that alley."

"I'm going to East 108th and look around," she told the desk sergeant. "Bring me back a hamburger," he said.

Although not on the force as long as most of those attached to Chicago homicide, Julia knew a front-page case when she saw it. What had this attractive young man in his well-worn Italian suit and tie been doing in a remote alleyway on the Southside? There were no hints of drugs or other motives to bring diverse cultures together in the middle of the night. Had he been killed somewhere else and dragged to the scene? She trusted the final crime scene report would tell her more.

She parked the squad car near the scene and buttoned up the collar of her heavy blue coat against the April winds bustling in from Lake Michigan a half mile away. She went door to door through and around the several blocks she'd circled, its center the back alleyway where the body had been found.

Some of the houses in the neighborhood were empty, or its inhabitants had better things to do than to speak with a police officer. Mostly women came to the door, kids banging around and making noise in other parts of their homes. The women looked at the photograph, then at her, back again at the photo, and shook their heads.

The dead man's fingerprints were unmatched in all the usual places. The lab reckoned he was in his mid-twenties, but his description didn't point at anyone reported missing. No rings on his fingers, only a slight depression on the third finger of his right hand where he might have worn a school ring. The labels had been cut out of his clothes. There was nothing in his pockets and no cell phone or Blackberry device. Whoever had seen him last hadn't wanted anyone else to know his identity . . . not for a while, anyway. The scene and his condition suggested to Julia that he'd been dragged into that alley and left for someone to find.

Julia knew the young man in the crime lab would be missed. Somewhere, a young woman about her age would leave another message on his answering machine, a boss would become more agitated by the minute, a dog would finally give up and urinate on the arm of the living room couch, or a child would wait to be taken to school or picked up at the bus station. And, lest Julia forget, a mother might wonder why her child hadn't called.

When you murder someone, why make it easy? But what do you do with all the things that could reveal the path of life this guy had traveled? Labels were hard to remove from shoes. So, take them off. Forget the socks. He doesn't need his feet warmed.

"Maybe the bare feet were all that was real," another said, "and the suit and tie were the cover up."

She laughed. Probably the killer couldn't get the labels out of the man's shoes.

Julia's preliminary analysis of the Southside killing consisted of one negative point. She'd arrived there early, but she couldn't move beyond it.

"I'm certain it was not a mugging in the street sense," she told Chief Donovan.

"The wallet was gone," he said.

"True, but look at the crime scene photos. When was the last time we found a victim with his arms crossed . . . the way a body is placed in a casket . . . and with his suit coat buttoned up like a mother would dress her kid for school? No guy I've ever known would button up his jacket like that. And where was his overcoat? Hell, the only thing missing was a flower in his hand."

"My guess is some kids or a homeless person came by, found him, and took his overcoat, wallet, cell phone, and shoes . . . ."

The chief wasn't paying attention. "You think?" she said, moving sideways to make direct eye contact with him. "Did they rip all the labels out of his clothes and cart him back into that alley to make people laugh?"

Donovan tuned in to what she was saying. "Unless he was looking for drugs or some bimbo to give him satisfaction."

"Okay, Chief, but if you saw the body in the lab . . . I don't think this guy was on drugs, and with looks and a *bod* like that, he didn't need to go to the Southside to get . . . what'd you call it . . . 'satisfaction'?"

Chief Donovan laughed hard. "All right, Gold," he said, still laughing, "but let's treat this as routine for as long as we can. The only time I find trouble around this place is when I try to make a big deal out of an ordinary 'take the money and run' hit."

Chief Detective Donovan liked Julia Gold, both as a good police officer and as an attractive young woman. She knew what he thought, but she did nothing to cultivate his preference. She didn't date within the force. That was based on some good advice she'd received from the man who taught her about life, her father.

She missed her father and his broad shoulders. He'd taught her to believe in herself, and he'd given her the confidence to meet challenges head on. No lectures. Instead, he'd offered examples and pointed to other peoples' successes and failures. He let her make up her own mind and come back to him for confirmation.

The stair climber and running machines at Julia's gym had the usual television programming to take boredom out of the process. She gazed absently at an old Cary Grant movie, while running up hill at five mph. Grant's on-the-screen girlfriend stuffed a card into his front coat pocket. His character had a handkerchief in that pocket, but the suit coat of the young man in the morgue, like most men's today, didn't.

On a hunch, she hopped off the treadmill and called the precinct on her cell phone. The sergeant on duty was a man she'd worked with before moving over to Homicide.

"Yeah, it's Julia, Mike. I need someone to check out the clothes we took off that dead guy who was picked up near East 108th Street."

"If his effects are still here. What d'ya want?"

"I assume we checked all his pockets."

"He had no I.D."

"I need someone to check again . . . the pocket on the front of his coat. You know . . . the one you guys put a kerchief in when you go to funerals and weddings."

She heard him grunt at the other end of the line. "You think?" the sergeant said.

"Do you mind? It's a long shot."

"Sure, call dispatch in an hour."

"Busy night, huh?"

"Isn't it always?"

"Look, I'll come down. If you have someone dig his stuff out of the evidence lockup, I'll sign out for it when I get there."

"Okay, Gold. See you later then."

Good old Alfred Hitchcock, her dad's favorite moviemaker. Julia had no doubt her dad had engineered the whole thing from on high. As soon as she saw the suit coat, she knew she'd find something in that pocket.

Embedded into the fabric inside the pocket, from the heat of more than one cleaning, she found the remains of a business card emblazoned on the front side with the faded logo of a financial institution in Manhattan. The writing on the backside of the card, which had not been ironed into the fabric, had been penned with a flare . . . by a young woman, she thought. With the help of ultraviolet light Julia worked most of it out:

"B[....]h Ta[...]r

2[..]4 East 7[....]

Apt. [..]5E

21[.]-66[...]58."

Both her department and the killer had missed it. Maybe she'd get lucky again and find a person to fill in the blanks at the company whose faded logo appeared on the front of the card. New York City was a long way out of her jurisdiction. She'd either have to bring in the FBI or the NYPD. Either way, she would need the chief's okay.

Julia didn't like working alone at her desk at night . . . the thinness of air not penetrated by sunlight and the frequency of involuntary visits to police headquarters by persons who needed the cover of darkness to manage their lives. She placed the card in a plastic sandwich bag, and left it in her locked desk drawer. She went to meet friends who shared the box at Wrigley Field her father had put in her name before his death. No baseball that day, but a few beers, and maybe a hug or two, was always a possibility.

The next morning she opened up her desk before Chief Donovan arrived in the office. She tried filling in the faded letters in the name written on the back of the card. "Tanner" fit the letters she'd worked out and seemed the best possibility. With an hour time difference in her favor, she made an anonymous call to the firm named on the front side of the business card, and confirmed that a woman named Beth Tanner still worked there.

She waited for Donovan to finish his coffee, knocked on his closed door, and placed the business card she'd found on his desk. She gave the previous night's duty officer credit for the discovery.

"Have you tried calling the New York department?"

"Do you think that's what we should do? What about the FBI?"

"No FBI," Donovan said. "Not yet, anyhow."

"When I call the NYPD, do I tell them I'm coming or let them make the contact?"

"Why not, if she's there?"

"I'd like to meet her in the flesh, like I would if she was here in town."

Donovan peered at her with his head turned down. He glanced back at the card, and flipped it over in his hand. "You found the card. Now go find her. I want to know who this guy was."

"Thanks, Chief," and she headed back to her desk.

"Gold," he called after her. "Remember . . . everyone's involved until you exclude them. I've a good contact on the NYPD. Want me to call him?"

She felt apprehensive about venturing into another city's precincts, especially New York. She turned and nodded, wondering at the same time why he'd felt it necessary to tell her not to exclude anyone from the investigation. Hell, there wasn't anyone to exclude. They didn't even know who this guy was.

"Okay, give me a few minutes," Donovan said.

"Yes, sir."

The New York sergeant's call back to Julia confirmed that a woman named Beth Tanner still worked at the bank, a fact that she'd already worked out.

"Do you want to be with us when we interview her?" the voice asked.

"Ms. Tanner needs to see this business card. I'll bring it with me," she said, answering the question in a manner she thought made objection to her accompanying them more difficult.

"You could send it here," the man said.

"I'm not letting this card out of my sight, Sergeant. It's the only thing we have. We'll need this woman's help, and my chief wants the body identified. We have an idea this homicide might have pretty wide implications."

She heard resignation in the sergeant's voice. "When can we expect you, Detective?"

"I'll be on the next flight into LaGuardia."

"Okay, come directly to the precinct station house on East 51st. The cab driver will know where it is. Ask for Sergeant Bernard. By the way, are you bringing in the Feds?"

"Not yet. We don't know what the crime was, or even if there was a crime. Maybe this Tanner woman can shed some light on it. Until then, we're treating it as a local matter."

"Good," the sergeant said.

"Yes, stay overnight," Donovan agreed. "But I want to know where and how you are, Gold, and watch yourself. New York is not as friendly a town as Chicago."

"I guess our victim didn't find it very friendly here, Chief."

Donovan laughed. "Okay, but I mean it. We have enough people down in this division, I don't need another."

She was happy not to be making the round trip in one day. Hopefully, they'd interview Tanner that afternoon, and she'd have the extra time as a failsafe. If she were lucky enough to obtain a few leads to the man's purpose for being in Chicago, it would move the investigation forward. She was in high spirits arriving at O'Hare, looking forward to her first official visit to the Big Apple and the discovery of the elusive identity.

MANHATTAN ISLAND

Beth Tanner dressed expensively and spoke Eastern establishment. She answered the New York police sergeant's questions in a clear, pleasant tone, fully enunciating every syllable as she might when speaking into a microphone. If she felt nervous about being interviewed by two plain-clothed police persons in a conference room at her place of employment, it was not apparent to Julia.

"It was at the Museum of Modern Art," Tanner said. "The bank held a cocktail party there for some charitable benefit. I think it was for children with MS . . . not sure about that, but I do remember him."

"That was almost two years ago," the police sergeant said with more bite in his voice than Julia thought she would've used.

The young woman either missed the doubt in the policeman's voice or chose to ignore it. "Absolutely," she said. "If you can wait a couple of minutes I'll get my little red book." She left and came back in ten minutes with a small notebook.

"Sorry, I bumped into my boss in the hall," she said in a cheery voice, and opened the little red book to the address section inside the back cover. "Arnold is not so common a name that I'd forget," she said, pointing to the spot where she'd written it down. "I was at the museum early, helping to set things up. I saw him come in, and knew right then I had to meet him."

Julia didn't blame her.

"When did you give him your card?" the sergeant asked.

"He had people surrounding him by the time I was free to move around. I finally managed to introduce myself. We talked for a while before I was called away. I wrote my home address and telephone number on that card before getting back to him . . . you know . . . just in case," she said, winking at Julia.

Julia smiled, acknowledging the point.

The sergeant cleared his throat. "Did he ever call you?"

Beth Tanner was on a roll. "We were having a really good conversation. I was getting good vibes there, if you know what I mean. He had the most gorgeous way of tilting his head when he spoke to you," she said, again looking to Julia as if she'd understand better. "Then some pushy older woman came running up and took over. I think they'd known each other, not sure, but she was a real bitch, all wrapped up in suburban glitter. That's the trouble with those really nice guys. They don't have to chase after women, but they're sitting ducks for overly aggressive females. Anyway, I had to leave. So I stuck the card in his pocket and gave his arm a squeeze. He winked at me, but maybe he didn't realize I'd put the card there. Maybe he forgot. Anyway, he never called."

"Which pocket did you put the card in?" The sergeant asked.

"This one," she said, pointing at the front pocket on her own jacket.

"Did the other woman give her name?" he asked.

Beth Tanner shook her head. "I don't know who she was. Never saw her again. I never saw him again either, and his name wasn't on the guest list. I had no way of getting in touch with him, although he did tell me he worked for the *Times*. I don't know if that was a line or not, but it didn't seem like he needed to spin yarns to get dates."

"Was that the *New York Times*?" Julia asked.

"That's where he said he worked. See," she said, pointing at her penciled notes, which read "*Times* - Paris."

"What's the Paris about?" Julia asked.

"Oh, sorry, he said he worked in Paris for the *Times*."

"And you're sure his name was Judd Arnold?"

The woman nodded, still showing a residue of annoyance at having been preempted by the person she'd called a "bitch." "Here," she said, showing Julia her little red book. "You can see where I wrote his name down."

Julia wanted be sure of the time line. "That was nineteen months ago?"

"Yes, amazing, but it was. I remember him as if it were yesterday. I guess I was impressed, eh?" she said, mocking herself with a gentle laugh. The woman's face suddenly became sad. "What was he doing in Chicago that got him killed?" she asked Julia.

"So this is the famous *New York Times*," Julia Gold said as she walked through the lobby in the company of the New York police officer assigned to assist her during her brief stay in Manhattan. She appreciated how much having the NYPD along facilitated her visit. He handled the security desk at the *Times* in seconds.

"They're expecting us upstairs," the officer said, and he led the way to the elevator.

A *Times* vice president paced the floor, listening to Julia's questions. What was Judd Arnold doing on the Southside of Chicago? He didn't have a clue.

"You understand, Detective," the *Times* representative said to Julia, "we don't have direct responsibility for the *Trib*. It's part of the company, and we refer to it as the *Times* international edition, but we're not structurally the same newspaper."

"Can you put us in touch with anyone who might have some idea what Mr. Arnold was working on that brought him to Chicago?" Julia asked.

The *Times* VP took a thin book from one of his desk drawers and opened it. He wrote several names on the pad on his desk and handed the page to her. "You can start here with these two in Washington. I'm sure they can at least point you in the right direction. I can call them for you right now if you'd like."

Julia nodded. The VP picked up his phone and called a number in their Washington office. When he had the right person on the line, he handed the phone to Julia.

She mouthed her thanks and took the phone. "This is Detective Gold, and I appreciate your taking the time to speak with me."

"Certainly, Detective, can you give me the reporter's name again."

"Judd Arnold. We believe him to be the person who was found dead in Chicago last week. We have no photo I.D. for him, but we have reason to believe he worked for the *International Herald Tribune*. If you have someone by that name you might send us a photo. We're also not certain exactly what his job was with your organization. We'd settle at this point for some employment records or next of kin."

"I can check that name for you, Detective. I guess you need it as soon as possible."

"Yes, Sir, we sure do."

"Well, it's almost midnight in Paris, but I have an idea. Where will you be in about an hour? The photo should be no problem if I come up with the name."

Julia and her NYPD escort were given a tour of the *Times* while they waited for the return call from Washington. She hadn't realized how much technology was involved in getting out a newspaper. She still had images of typesetting machines and editors with green eyeshades, but what she saw were computers and a lot of t-shirts.

The call back, when it came, provided more information than Julia had expected or hoped for.

"Judd Arnold does indeed work for the *Tribune* in Paris . . . or did, I guess I should say. In fact, he was here in Washington recently on assignment. Apparently, everyone here thought he'd gone back to Paris after visiting his family. If the staff in Paris is looking for him, they haven't briefed us. When did you say his body was found?"

"Early morning on the sixth."

The caller spoke as he searched his records. "He might have gone from here to Chicago then. He was at our office here in D.C. on the fourth."

"On assignment you said . . . from Paris?" Julia asked.

"Yes, he was here on an assignment that took him to New Orleans, but not Chicago. I took the liberty of asking around to those who might have a better idea of what he was working on, and no one thinks Chicago was involved in anything he was doing. He knew some of the guys here from the time he was on his familiarization tour . . . before he was moved to Paris. He told them he was working on a human-interest piece connecting the *Frenchness* of New Orleans to the people of France. They all had a big laugh about it."

Julia didn't ask what the joke was. "Are there people I can talk with down there, or am I better off dealing directly with his office in Paris?"

"Well, you're a much better judge of that than I, Detective, but I can tell you that Arnold's parents live right there in New York. Maybe you can get some help from them. Do they know he's dead? One of the men here thought Judd was going to visit his parents before returning to Paris."

"Do you have their number?"

"Sorry, I don't, but they live in Hempstead, Long Island. I've arranged for his photo to be sent to you at the number you gave me. I will also send the names of Paris editorial staff you could speak with in the morning. I'm sure they can tell you more about what Judd Arnold was working on."

"Thank you very much," Julia said, and suddenly remembering another question, "Would Judd Arnold have had a company cell phone?"

"Yes. Probably, but probably not one that would work here in the U.S. I'm sure you know that the European system is different."

Julia looked at the NYPD sergeant and hunched her shoulders, saying in effect she guessed everyone knew that, didn't they. The sergeant smiled back. Then, she telephoned Chief Donovan in Chicago.

"I think we've identified the dead guy. He worked for the *New York Times* in Paris. We haven't made that contact yet, but his parents live out on Long Island."

"Okay, Gold. You're cleared to speak with the man's parents since you're already there. Are you going to take the NYPD with you?"

"Do I have to? Seems like overkill. I'd like to handle it my way."

"All right. If the parents raise a fuss, have them call me. You're not plan-ning a trip to Paris too, are you?" he asked.

Julia heard the humor in his voice. "No sir, Chief. I figured you'd like to make that trip."

"I don't *parlay* French, Gold. Just find out what in hell the man was doing in Chicago. I hope to God that neither one of us has to go to Paris for that."

"Chief, this is getting curiouser and curiouser."

"You got that right, Gold. Get back here tomorrow."

HEMPSTEAD, NY

"Yes, good morning. You must be the policewoman from Chicago."

No, I'm the Good Humor Man. The combination of impatience and not wanting to be there got her off to a bad start, and nerves converged to test her. She kept those thoughts to herself, smiled, and nodded.

"Please come in," Judd's mother said.

"Thank you. I'm Detective Gold, Mrs. Arnold. I'm sorry to be here under these circumstances." Her words trailed off as Judd's mother turned her back and was five strides ahead, leading the way through a small kitchen and into a stuffy dining room where their meeting was set to take place.

Julia followed, dutifully recalling her boss' last words, "Keep 'em happy, Gold." *That was not going to be easy.*

She could see that the young man in the photographs on tables and in cubicles around the Arnold home resembled his mother and matched the photo she'd received from the *Times.* Ad Arnold had the same striking dark eyes and curly, jet black hair, complimenting a milk white complexion. The father was rounder and quite ordinary looking in Gold's eyes, but his personality was less abrasive than his wife's. She wondered which version of these juices had run through their son's veins.

"I'm so sorry to be here under . . . " she began as David Arnold handed her a cup of coffee and she took a seat at the dining table. "I thought perhaps we could put our heads together and figure out what your son was doing in Chicago. If we knew the answer, we might find out what happened."

"Humph," Judd's mother said, rejoining them at the table. "Where again exactly did this happen, Detective?"

"Your son's body was found in an alleyway near East 108th Street on the south side of town."

"Who found him?" Ad Arnold shot back.

"My precinct, following up on an anonymous phone call."

"What time of day?"

"It was around one-thirty Tuesday morning, April sixth," she said, letting the Arnolds carry the ball . . . less chance of stumbling into something that might upset them anymore than they were.

"Why are you just telling us now?" David Arnold asked.

Julia had prepared for this question. She cleared her throat. "That's a fair question, Mr. Arnold. Judd had no identification on him. Even the labels were ripped out of his clothes."

"But you did identify him?" the father asked, showing very little belief in what he was hearing, and possibly, Julia thought, hoping his son was still alive.

"There was a woman's business card in his handkerchief pocket. We missed it first time through because it had partially melted into the fabric of his suit coat."

Ad Arnold produced a severe stare that shouted "incompetents" as Julia continued. "We traced this woman to a bank in Manhattan, and discovered that your son worked for the *Times*. They gave us your contact information."

"You've never found his wallet, or anything?" David asked.

"No."

"All the usual suspects? That didn't turn up anything?"

"Not so far," she said. Then, taking advantage of a lull in the questions coming, she returned to her theme. "We need to know what your son was doing in Chicago."

That charged up Ad Arnold, who blurted out, "Why the hell are you asking me? Ask the *New York Times* . . . or that Franco rag of theirs. He should never have gone to work for them. I told you, David, that no good would come of it. Now, he's gone." With the back of one hand she wiped away the tears that were streaming down her face.

"Did he travel often here to the U.S. in his work?" Julia asked.

"We don't know what he does," the mother answered, "except take those trips down to Washington to see that old girlfriend of his. She's the cause of all this. I tell you that right now."

"Now, Ad, we don't know that he even called Katherine when he traveled on business to Washington." He turned to Julia. "You see, Detective Gold, Judd was enrolled at the Law School at Georgetown University. Shortly after going back for his second year, he left school and spent time in Manhattan and in Paris, living off the tuition money we gave him until he landed the job in Paris with the *International Herald Tribune*."

Arnold raised his hand to his wife as she started to interrupt, and continued. "It was late in the fall of that year when we found out he was moving to Paris to work at the newspaper. During all those weeks, whenever we tried contacting him at the number he'd given us, a woman whose name is Katherine Stevens answered. He'd call us back, usually a day or so later. When the university wrote and asked why we hadn't paid his tuition, we realized this girl had been covering for him."

Julia looked back at Judd's mother. She knew her next question was a dangerous one in the woman's present state, but she nonetheless asked, "Why do you think this young woman . . ." She checked her notes for the name. " . . . Katherine Stevens . . . would know anything about your son's death? Did they remain friends?"

This time, it was Adelaide Arnold who took a deep breath. "She's the reason Judd left law school."

Her husband coughed, covering his mouth with a hand. Julia waited, showing she expected a little more information.

"She was a slut. She'd played tennis at Stanford. Judd thought that made her something special, but she was just a slut. I told her she should be very proud, always keeping Judd's whereabouts from the people who really loved him."

They both waited as Ad Arnold collected herself.

"Where can I reach this woman?" Gold asked.

Ad Arnold nodded, went into her desk, returned with her address book, and looked up Stevens' telephone number.

"Thank you, Mrs. Arnold," Julia said, noting the number on her day pad. "Do you also have a cell phone number for Judd?"

Ad Arnold's hand trembled as she leafed through to the page that contained her son's contact information. Julia noted this matched the one given her by the *Times* staff in Washington—the one which did not work in the U.S. She tucked both numbers away, and wondered if the chief would authorize her to take a trip to Washington, D.C. The victim's mother was overreacting for sure, but Julia had seldom seen such abject hatred coming out of anyone. She needed to check out this Stevens woman—the sooner the better.

THE WATERGATE

Katherine Stevens' professional life, expansive and limitless when she got up that morning, became compressed by uncertainty and the fear that comes with it. She brushed back the lock of blond hair that fell across her right eye whenever she felt stress, and gazed absently across the courtyards below toward the Kennedy Center and along the Potomac River. The tennis ball she imagined tossing and hitting again and again against a backboard faded into nothingness and would not bounce back.

She was too inwardly focused to hear the door to their apartment open and her mate throw off his coat in the hall closet. Her own jacket was still on the floor at her feet on top of her briefcase, where she'd thrown both a half hour before. The notebook she kept on her desk was unopened in front of her, and she leaned back in her chair with her long legs stretched out, feeling like she'd just run a seven-minute mile.

She glanced up as the man she was going to marry came through the door to their study. He carried two glasses of wine, handed one to her and sat across from her on the loveseat they sometimes used for the named purpose.

Gordon could see Supreme Court Justice Goode's collapse in Chambers that morning had caught up with Kate. He raised his glass to hers.

Kate gave him a weak smile. "I miss him already, Gordon. Do you think he's coming back?"

"Tell me what happened."

Kate took a sip of her wine. "*Goodie* was standing by his bookcase when I went in to ask him a question. He turned when he heard me and started to say something, but his eyes got big, like he'd just caught something in his throat and couldn't breathe. Then he just folded over and fell to the floor. We were all asked not to leak it. I wanted to call you. Sorry."

"Does he know you call him Goodie?" he said with a twinkle in his eye.

His reward was the beginning of a smile. "That moniker came from some lady mispronouncing his name at a cocktail party benefit during the holidays. She didn't honor the silent "'e'" at the end. Since then, that's his name, among the law clerks, anyway," Kate said with an amused crinkle of her nose.

"How's the environment in Chambers?"

"*Goodie* was well liked," Kate said. "I think we all miss him. My alleged male friends asked me when I first noticed I had this effect on judges."

Gordon laughed. "Not just judges."

This earned a broader smile. "How did you get the news?" Kate asked.

"Charles Black called me."

Kate questioned him with her eyes.

"The White House heard the man will probably retire," he responded.

"Had Charles spoken with the President?"

"You mean about a potential replacement?"

Kate raised her chin ever so slightly, turning the wine glass in her hand. He knew she was back. "The President has two or three candidates in mind."

"Any idea who they might be?"

"Charles didn't say, and I didn't ask. She makes up her own mind on these things . . . and then tests reactions. They may leak it to the press and see what kind of reactions come in. Charles may call me at that point."

Kate shook her head. "You know you're going to be right in the middle of this once it gets going."

"We'll see," he said, standing up. "Now, how about if I rustle up some dinner while you get comfortable?"

Kate Stevens' first weeks clerking for Justice Goode at the United States Supreme Court mirrored some of her experiences on the fourteen-and-under national tennis circuit. Being new and an attractive female in this world is not without its drawbacks, whether swatting tennis balls in the Palo Alto sunshine or researching points of law at the United States Supreme Court. This time she was prepared. When she first pulled out the stops in a session with Justice Goode and his other law clerks, the effect was as dramatic as her cross-court winners on the tennis court. In both cases her protagonists had little choice but to accept her for the impressive talent she brought to their stage.

Casually and around town, Kate's persona was shared or diluted, depending upon your point of view, by the company of her fiancé, Gordon Cox. He was her hawk-eyed pass to the world inside the Beltway, and she savored being accepted as an equal who just happened to be attractive. In the culture of their home Gordon was easy-going yet expansive, and she adored him. "We're made for each other," she'd told her mother.

Gordon agreed with that assessment. He'd lived alone for nine years in the two units he'd combined on the top floor of The Watergate to form the rambling apartment that he and Kate now called home. During that time he'd become accomplished at practicing law in Washington, D.C., watched an old history professor get elected President, and prepared countless gourmet meals for himself and his guests. He'd had one or two serious relationships with the opposite sex, but from across the room at least he was not coated with honey, and more than one woman had found the kitchen too small for two cooks. In any case, no one before Kate had been offered marriage or invited to move in on any other premise.

Kate brightened and anchored Gordon's life. He could close his eyes and see clearly the bright, attractive, young law student that had walked into the firm three years before to begin a summer association. Kate had been taken from him by force that summer in Havana, and following her rescue and survival of a storm at sea they'd been inseparable. Clients, law partners, and the White House took up 60-plus hours of his normal week, but his love affair with Kate Stevens placed all the rest in perspective. She mattered, and together they were a force.

COLD SPRING RAIN

"Exactly what do you expect to accomplish in Washington, Gold?" Chief Donovan asked. "It's the last place I would go to find the truth about anything."

Julia nodded and smiled at his humor. "We're not getting anywhere with this Arnold killing. I can't close the door on it without interviewing the woman who, according to the victim's parents, was involved in at least one conspiracy together with their son. She may be the answer to what the man came here to do. The mother's still pointing her finger at this woman every time she calls downstairs, and we've got to check it out. I'd like to head back to New York to round out a few details the NYPD is collecting for us. I'll take the train down to D.C. and fly back from there. Two days is all I'll need."

"If it will get that damn Arnold woman off our backs . . . okay . . . go."

"She's a real piece of work."

"That lady has called the mayor, the commissioner and both of the Illinois senators."

"Is that why the senator is suddenly so interested?"

"Sure. He's looking for an angle to get his face on television. That woman has him convinced of some big conspiracy between her son and this young woman and others in Washington. That young woman, by the way, is a lawyer in Washington, and one of legal eagles told the commissioner she's a law clerk for a justice on the Supreme Court. So tread carefully with her. And you'd better find out the rest of what our *legals* know before you head east."

"This is getting very political, Chief."

"Yeah, you should let the Legal Department handle it. You'll get caught in between, and believe me it will not be fun if you do."

Julia didn't take him seriously. "Okay," she said, "I'll hear what the *legals* have on this woman. I told you this case was going to be interesting."

"Humph," Donovan said as Julia got out of the chair and went back to her desk.

The wet spring storm she encountered on the Amtrak trip to Washington from Manhattan was a minor inconvenience for Julia Gold. The floor in the back seat of the Washington taxi was wet, and she had to shuffle through puddles when her time came to climb into the cab in front of Union Station for the ride out to Georgetown.

She'd made a hotel reservation there in the mistaken belief that Georgetown Law School was near the primary undergraduate campus. She discovered the next morning that she could have walked a few blocks from the train station to the Georgetown Legal Center and Law School buildings, which stand within the springtime shadows cast by Capitol Hill.

The law school's records, when she finally arrived, didn't reveal much about Judd Arnold. His first year grades were above average, surprisingly good for someone who didn't want to be in law school in the first place. She expected to find worse. His attendance record, such as was available, appeared to be excellent. Not all professors held to strict attending procedures, and most on the faculty could not place his name or face. He certainly did not make an impact, good or bad, in the one year he'd spent at the school.

In contrast, the name of the woman the dead man's mother had given her to contact was well-known and fondly remembered. She was also close by. Everything she'd been shown about this Katherine Stevens gave Julia the impression she was a bright, pretty woman . . . which in Julia's neck of the woods spelled *soft and probably spoiled rotten*. She decided to play on that melody by being cold and direct. *Let's see what you're all about, Ms. Stevens,* she mumbled to herself, and contacted Kate at her clerk's cubicle in the Supreme Court chambers.

"Ms. Stevens, my name is Julia Gold. I'm with the Chicago police department. I'm in town investigating an apparent homicide. Could you come over to the Law Center? I have a room here."

Gold watched a blond woman about her own age bound up the steps into the school forum where she sat. The woman entered the hall and approached Julia with an outstretched hand. They looked each other over as they shook hands and went behind closed doors into a room near the library.

"Thanks for coming over," Julia said.

"No problem, Detective. I'm right up top of the hill."

A little small talk to get the inquisition started. "This is my second time to Washington. The last time was with my parents when I was in second grade. I assumed the law school was out in Georgetown when I booked my hotel, so I took a long taxi ride this morning. I thought the driver was giving me the business."

Kate laughed. "A common error. You're not the first."

"So you work at the Supreme Court?"

"I'm one of Justice Goode's law clerks. I'm at the bottom of the pecking order over there."

"Must be an honor though."

"Yes, it's an honor," Kate said with a tight smile. "I'm lucky to be here."

"You earned it from what they tell me around here."

Kate blushed, and shrugged her shoulders.

Julia rushed in with all her antennas focused . . . *from Legal Land on the top of Capitol Hill, she joked to herself. We'll see how she handles a good old-fashioned Chicago police whupping.*

"I was in New York last week interviewing Adelaide and David Arnold. I believe you know them and their son, Judd."

Kate nodded that she did, and waited for the other shoe to drop.

"Judd Arnold was murdered in Chicago a couple of weeks ago, Ms. Stevens. Were you aware of that?"

Kate never took her eyes off her. "I didn't know that," she said, swallowing and partially choking on the saliva in her throat.

Julia looked at her as Kate took a tissue from her bag and blew her nose.

"How well did you know Judd Arnold, Ms. Stevens?"

"Judd is dead?"

"Yes. He was killed. We found his body on the Southside of Chicago."

Kate nodded, but seemed unwilling to trust her voice.

"How well did you know Judd Arnold, Ms. Stevens?"

"We were good friends. We spent time together the first year here at the law school. He was only back at school a few days the following year before he left."

Julia set up her first test. "Odd . . . his father told me Judd didn't leave school until November."

Kate uncrossed and re-crossed her legs, cleared her throat, and said more forcefully, "He left after the first week. It was in September. I don't think his parents knew until later."

Undeterred, Julia bored in. "How could that be? I got the impression the Arnolds were quite close as a family." If this didn't sweat out the truth, Gold knew she had an unreliable witness.

Kate took a deep breath and nodded. "Judd asked me to cover for him until he got a job. He wanted to be a reporter, and he intended to make the rounds, looking for a newspaper job."

"Why do you think he asked you?" It didn't sound so innocent to Julia.

"I don't think he had many really close friends here, and he and I were in the same study group first year. We got along well. I don't know . . . I guess he just trusted me," Kate said.

Julia squinted and leaned over close to Kate. "Trust is an interesting word. It wasn't a very nice thing to do, conspiring with the man against his own mother."

"No, I guess it wasn't," Kate said after a short pause. "But the circumstances seemed to make it right. I never dreamed it would go on for as long as it did."

"What circumstances?"

Julia was almost nose-to-nose with Kate at this point. She could see this unnerved her witness a bit, but any idea that Kate Stevens would melt was quickly dismissed. Kate raised her chin and spoke in clear tones, as Julia thought she might when talking to a judge. "Judd's mother was going to be very upset at his leaving the study of law. He wanted to have a good job all set before he was forced to tell her. You need to understand, Detective, that Mrs. Arnold is a strong personality, and she had very definite plans for Judd. He knew he couldn't stand up to her, so he just didn't tell her."

"And left you to cover for him. Why did you do it? Did you do it to get even with his mother? How did Mrs. Arnold know to call you?"

Kate shook her head, but it wasn't clear to Julia to which question her headshake was a response. "Judd wrote a letter, telling his mother he was doing a project at school with me, that I had my own phone, and she could reach him through me in a pinch . . . something like that."

"Didn't he have a mobile phone?"

"I don't think so."

It all sounded contrived to Julia . . . like it had been rehearsed. "So, Mrs. Arnold must have thought you two were living together."

"That's probably right."

"And sleeping in the same bed, no doubt."

For the first time, Julia thought, she'd gotten through. This had clearly pushed a button.

Kate said nothing for a moment or two . . . just looked straight at Julia. Then, she smiled . . . almost laughed. "In my short time dealing with mothers of boys who were trying to get their hands up my skirt, I'd say Mrs. Arnold fit the pattern almost exactly."

"So, did she call?"

Kate tossed her head, and this time really did laugh. "Did she call? I'll say she called, and christened me with every four letter word in the book, as well as some that aren't in the book."

Julia tried hard not to laugh with Kate. "How did they finally find out where he was?"

"I think it was around mid-October when I got the first call. They'd tried to reach him for a few weeks I guess before that, but not more than three or four weeks passed from the time I received the first call until he told them he had a job with the *Herald Tribune* in Paris."

"I thought you said his mother called a lot."

"She did, but most of it was after they knew the truth. She blamed me for his leaving law school."

"You know that she blames you now for what happened to her son in Chicago. She has told my department that she's sure you were involved in whatever it was he was doing, and that we should obtain a warrant to go through your computer for evidence. If it comes to that would you be willing to cooperate?"

Kate stared at her. "You can't believe that nonsense."

"It's not a question of what I believe or don't believe. She's made this accusation. I've got to check it out."

"You know, Detective, that the negative is always difficult to prove, but I can tell you that I haven't seen or spoken with Judd Arnold in over a year and that we were not involved . . . ever . . . in any exercise or activity of any nature outside of law school."

Julia had to admit at first impressions that Kate was slightly more reliable than Mrs. Arnold. She changed directions. "So, what was Judd Arnold like?" she asked.

"That . . . I can help you with. He was bright, tenacious, and had a great sense of humor."

"Were you two . . . ?"

"Lovers?"

"Yeah."

"No."

Julia didn't find that answer believable. Ad Arnold had told everyone who would listen that her son and Kate Stevens were sexually involved, and Julia found that easy to believe. Julia's raised eyebrows gave her thoughts away.

"No, it's true. We never got that involved. If we'd been at school in California, or some other place more than a couple of hours by train from his mother, things might have developed. We really liked each other. There was some touching, but there was no magic there, especially after his mother came into the picture."

Julia proceeded to put Mrs. Arnold's theory to the test. "Ms. Stevens, please forgive me, but didn't you ever see the man naked? He was dead when I saw him lying on a slab in the police morgue, but I have to tell you if I'd been in Judd Arnold's study class, I'd have been all over him. I would have had a go. You can tell me the truth. There's no connection with sex to his murder, but you've got to level with me."

Kate straightened up and flushed. "We were not lovers, Detective Gold." She paused a moment before regaining some composure. "I agree with you, he was good-looking, and a nice person to boot, fun to be with, but we were not involved beyond a pass he made one night, like it was expected of him, when we'd both had a couple of drinks . . . not lovers, just good friends."

Julia wasn't satisfied. "It's not that I don't believe you, Ms. Stevens, it's just that I don't understand it. You would have seemed perfect for each other." Then, she stopped suddenly, courtesy of an intruding thought. "He was Jewish, wasn't he? Is that what was wrong?"

Kate frowned, but maintained eye contact. "No, but I wasn't looking for romance my first year at law school. I'd spent the previous ten years playing tennis all over the country and being hit on from age fourteen by half the males, and some of the females, I met along the way. Sex was hardly a stranger to the college tennis circuit. I promised myself it would not happen in law school. The fact that other people might have thought Judd and I were an item helped keep others at arm's length that first year, so I did nothing to throw cold water on the appearance. That's all. It wasn't Judd. It was me . . ." and Kate paused . . . "except . . ."

Julia loved the word, "except." She perked up whenever she heard it. "Except? What?"

"Judd had played a lot of amateur tennis with his mother. He was pretty good, and I guess his mother was very good . . ."

"But you beat him."

"He hadn't practiced and played in competition from age eight like I had. Tennis is not a social game to me."

She was starting to understand this woman. "I guess that'll cool down a young man's testosterone," Julia said.

Kate acknowledged the point, and for the first time showed a friendly smile. "I think it was more like both his mother and I were good in the same sport. It was definitely a turn-off. Also, I don't think either of us were up for the adverse impact his mother would have on our lives if he and I became an item. I'm sure Adelaide Arnold thought we were making out. I bet that's what she told you."

"That's a nice engagement ring," Julia said, pointing at Kate's finger and dodging the question implied by her statement.

"Thank you."

"When's the big event?"

"I'm afraid the court prefers its law clerks to be single. We haven't set a date. Anyway, we're having too much fun being engaged. We'll get around to it eventually, maybe when children start to enter the picture."

She nodded wistfully. She looked at Kate and spoke as she might to the sister she'd never had. "Do you have any idea what he might have been doing in Chicago last month? I have to tell you, Mrs. Arnold thinks you were with him or at least hatching up some kind of conspiracy."

"I didn't know he was in the country, let alone Chicago."

Julia watched as Kate started to say something, and then hesitated.

"What is it?"

"Exactly when did you discover Judd's body?"

Julia looked intently at Kate, and opened her notebook. "It was at 1:24 a.m. on a Tuesday morning. Why?"

"And the date, was it during the first part of April?"

"Yes," she said, looking squarely into Kate's eyes. "Why?"

"So he could have been in the country on Sunday the fourth?"

"In fact we know he was," Julia said. He was here in Washington on that date, having come in from New Orleans on an assignment. Why? What are you trying to tell me?"

"There was a call around seven in the evening on Sunday, the fourth. I remember because Gordon and I had just come in from a weekend in New York. Whoever it was hung up before I could get there."

"Did you redial?" Julia asked, always interested in phone numbers.

"Yes, but no one picked up. It had a New York prefix. We'd just come from there, so it was probably one of the people we visited up there."

"New York?"

"Yes."

"Do you still have it on your Blackberry?"

"I might," Kate said, scrambling to remove the Blackberry from its case.

Julia watched while Kate checked the call log. "I don't see any New York numbers left here anymore. I didn't save it. The timing is a bit coincidental. You think it might have been Judd Arnold?"

"Did Judd call often?" Gold asked.

"He lived in Paris."

The expression on Julia's face said, *answer the question, girl. Don't you know how important this is?* "When he was here in the States . . . did he call?"

"I told you. We hadn't spoken in well over a year."

Julia took a moment to reflect. "What does your fiancé do?"

"He's a lawyer."

"What's his name?"

"Gordon Cox."

Familiar, but Julia couldn't place it. "And you guys are living together?"

"Yes."

"Did Judd know you were engaged?"

"I sent him an announcement."

"To Paris?" she asked.

"No, I sent it to his parents' home on Long Island."

She didn't say anything right away, but Kate filled in the vacuum for her.

"I see where you're going, Detective. You think maybe he never got it."

She'd seen enough of Ad Arnold to know that was more than a possibility. "That's what I was thinking, Ms. Stevens. I guess he knew you were working for the Supreme Court, though."

"He might not have known that. The last time we spoke I was clerking over at the Court of Appeals. The justice I clerked for there recommended me to Justice Goode seven months ago."

"Well, okay. I guess we've beaten this old horse to death."

"Sorry."

"Yeah, I was hoping you'd be able to tell us why he went to Chicago." Thinking back to what Ad Arnold had told her, Julia crossed the line with Kate. "Why does Judd's mother dislike you so much? Does it all go back to your covering for him?"

Kate nodded. "My covering for him made it clear, I think, that Judd had left the roost. That Judd would conspire with another woman against her . . . wow; she had a hard time with that. I can only imagine how she feels about me now."

Julia closed the notebook in front of her on the table.

Kate seemed to take that as the sign that Julia intended. She used the tissue to blow her nose again. "Detective, may I call you to see how you're progressing on finding what happened to Judd?"

"Call me any time, Ms. Stevens. I may do the same. Maybe you'll think of something more. There are people out there who think Judd Arnold was involved doing more than just a story. If you and he were not doing something together, then maybe someone else was. I'd love to have you think about that. And . . . I'll need you to tell me where you were on the night of April sixth. When you do that, please also give the names of any persons who can verify your presence on that time and place. Here's my address and my private number. It rolls over to my cell if I don't pick up."

"Okay, Detective I'll get that off to you ASAP, and I'll call you if I come up with anything."

Both professional women leaned back and gave a virtual sigh. It had been an uneasy 90 minutes during which mettle showed more than truth, and a symmetry of goals was established. Julia came away satisfied with the effort, but frustrated by the lack of knowledge about Judd Arnold's intentions for visiting her city. Kate decided to let the meeting rest where it lay. She knew the detective would make a report of the substance of her answers, but for the moment Kate's instincts told her to keep all further thoughts to herself.

Tenacious, bright, and a joker. That means he had a good imagination, Julia thought, and sorted through those notions and others on the way to Reagan National Airport and aboard her flight back to Chicago. No one seemed to know what the man had been doing in Chicago. His employer said he was on an assignment, which had taken him to New Orleans. He'd had a one-night layover in Miami . . . had he run into something there? There were eight or nine days in New Orleans (to Julia, that seemed a long time to write a short article), and then two days in Washington where he apparently used the *Times* office to pull his story together. It was a pretty cloudy picture. *It did kinda smell of a conspiracy.*

Before typing up her notes at home that night, Julia googled Katherine Stevens. The search revealed more under Kate than Katherine, and showed that the young woman had been modest in describing her college tennis career.

THE WHITE HOUSE

The President had made up her list of candidates for the Supreme Court shortly after being sworn into office. Senators, constituents, members of her own political party and her favorite bipartisans, pressured by various interest groups, tried to put their own choices near or at the top of that list. She accepted all such requests for what they were, political attempts to shape the constitutional stage to their liking or that of their clients.

She had her own visions of what the stage on which constitutional issues were played out should look like. After all, she'd taught American History in both high school and at a major university, and thought she saw the issues with a clear view of what that history had taught anyone who would listen.

Included on her own list of *possibles* was a woman lawyer with whom the President had spent time during the primary campaign. She'd been impressed by the woman's intellect and her willingness to represent minorities, taking on the large corporations and her own government in the process. The woman seemed professionally fearless. All these qualities, which appealed to the President, were the same elements that would make Charles Black's job difficult if she became the President's choice. The woman's name made the first two cuts, and she remained the only female on the short list. At that point, the President advised her chief of staff that the time had come to involve Gordon Cox.

The White House free pass into Gordon Cox's office was through his assistant, Emily Harding. It didn't matter in what work he was engaged or with whom he was meeting, Emily would track him down.

He moved past Emily with a wink, received a smile in return, and took the call at his desk.

As was Charles Black's style, he spent no time on small talk and made extensive use of the royal "we," which was Black's design to prevent anyone from thinking his own opinions were any different from the President's. "We've put Joan Chatrier on the short list for the court, Gordon. Any thoughts?"

Gordon paused for a moment, picturing the woman in his mind. "She's on the young side; she's got a few on me, must be about 48," he said.

"Is that good or bad?" Black asked.

"What does the President have in mind?" Gordon nodded to Emily as she moved around from behind her desk and closed the door to his office. He had few secrets from his assistant. He trusted her. On the other hand, Emily knew when he was on with the White House his door should not be left open.

"That's not much younger than the chief justice was when he was sworn in, Gordon," Black said. "Anyway, we think the court could use a bit more youth. The rest of the country has forty-nine-year-olds in high office, why not the Supreme Court?"

"Joan will meet a lot of resistance from business," Gordon said, knowing very well from his firm's own experience how some of their clients had reacted to this woman's success in taking on big corporations.

"Does that surprise you coming from this White House?"

Gordon laughed at what he knew was an attempt at humor. "No, but what's the point?"

"Fair question from one of the persons we hope will help us get the right person on the court. We give this a high priority . . . so much so that we'll put our whole credibility on it."

The manner in which Charles made the statement, and his tone, which Gordon took as very defensive, surprised him, and he greeted it in silence.

"You think this candidate would be a mistake?" Charles Black challenged.

"Could be. Why is this one so special?"

"It's our first Supreme Court appointment. You know she has a deep interest in the Constitution, and that it needs a well-balanced court to assure it moves with the times."

"She'll get another chance . . . probably."

"And we will take them one case at a time. Can we count on you or not?"

There were many times in the days and weeks to come that Gordon wished he'd answered this question more candidly. "Of course," he said.

"Good. We'll listen to your advice too, Gordon . . . as we proceed."

"Does Joan know?" he asked, shifting in his chair to get more comfortable.

"Not yet. We thought you might feel her out for us?"

"Sure, but why me?" He leaned back in the chair and twirled a pencil through his fingers.

"We thought you two were friends."

"Not close friends. I haven't seen her in awhile, but I respect her for what she's accomplished professionally."

"Is that a two-way street?"

"We're not enemies."

"Good, then. We need you to draw her out a bit before we make the final cut. Would you mind?"

"It might be good timing for Joan, since her husband died last year." And, as he spoke the words, Gordon had a flash of regret. Andre Chatrier had become a client when he left the French Foreign Service to start up his own business in Washington. Andre and Joan had met for the first time in one of the firm's conference rooms while she stilled worked there. It seemed like yesterday.

"An unusual lady," Andre said with a subtle nod in Joan's direction as she left the room, her share of their work finished. "Where did she learn her French?"

"Her mother's from Martinique," Gordon said.

"Really?"

But that was only half of Andre's question.

"She's not married," he said.

It wasn't long thereafter that Andre Chatrier and Joan Roland became one of the more interesting couples in town.

"Do you think Joan Chatrier would stay the course and not leave after a few years?" Black asked him.

"I don't know," Gordon said, "but that's certainly a fair question."

"One of the reasons we want a younger than usual person is to provide a longer presence, over an extra generation maybe."

"Are you ready for me to ask her about that?"

"Yes, but we haven't made up our mind yet, so don't get Chatrier's hopes up."

"I'm sure Joan knows how the system works. I'll get back to you in a few days. Or are we in a hurry?"

"No point in dilly-dallying."

Gordon laughed. "You bet. I'll call her today, Charles."

"If she gives us the green light . . . ."

Kate sensed a new energy as she opened the door and entered their Watergate apartment. When she found him, Gordon sat at his side of their desk in the den, sorting through a pile of papers. Something was definitely up. Gordon usually left his work in the office.

"Homework?" she asked, unbuttoning the top of her coat and swishing off her scarf.

"Oh, hi, Darling . . . didn't hear you come in."

She moved around behind Gordon and wrapped her arms around his shoulders. "What's up?" she said, her chin resting atop his head as she looked down at the papers laid out in front of him.

Gordon turned and smiled up at her. "You're going to love this," he said. "She's asked me to vet one of her *possibles* for appointment to the court."

"See . . . my intuitions are never wrong." She beamed as she moved over and sat on the love seat, her coat still on and brief case in her lap. "So, who's the lucky guy?"

"Not a guy," Gordon answered. "Her name is Joan Chatrier. She used to be with the firm."

She was surprised. "The super plaintiff's lawyer?"

"Yes," Gordon said.

"Didn't she win that big case against the Interior Department?"

"That's the one. The media loved following her around the country. That always brought in calls from the Firm's corporate clients and various senators, who coveted those same clients as special interests, and none of that group bathed in Joan's successes."

"Where's she now?" Kate asked. "I have not heard about her recently."

Gordon put down the pen in his hand and looked at her. "Her husband died two years ago. She slowed down after that. His death was sudden, and it hit her pretty hard. He was a nice man . . . a client of mine. They met in my office when she was still with the firm. She's teaching a class at GW now."

"But a big time plaintiffs' lawyer on the Supreme Court?" she said. "How's that going to go over?"

"Joan might be a tough sell these days for that reason alone. The President hasn't made any choices yet."

Being this close to a subject of national importance . . . one that touched her own job with the court . . . was exciting, and the man she'd promised to marry was right in the middle of the selection process. *Good stuff, she thought,* as she slipped out of her coat. She moved over to her side of the large desk they shared, elbows on the tabletop, searching Gordon's expression for more information. "Where'd Chatrier go to law school?"

"Penn."

"So her clerks will probably come from the Halls of Ivy."

"Most likely, or your undergraduate alma mater," Gordon said. "She did some postgraduate study at Stanford."

"I'll be sorry to miss that."

"You should be around for the first couple of weeks at least."

She didn't think so, but hunched her shoulders. "So, what's Charles Black want my Gordon to do?" she asked, straightening and leaning back in her chair.

He laughed. "I conduct the *voir dire*. Charles sent his best to you, by the way."

"Greetings from the White House, that's heady stuff," she said, and a thought occurred to her as she rose to her feet. "That's real involvement. I'm wondering how the chief justice will view one of his newly at-large law clerks engaged to marry the White House advisor on Justice Goode's replacement?"

Gordon bit the corner of his lip. "There aren't many secrets in this town, Kate. You should tell him, but keep your powder dry until we see what happens. Chatrier may not be the President's choice."

She nodded as she walked around the desk, gave him a hug, and dropped a letter on the table for him to see. "It's a note from Justice Goode. He sent one to each of his clerks, and they were all different. He did it right, didn't he?"

> *Dear Katherine,*
>
> *I'm sorry to cut short your time at court. The good Lord gave me a warning, and I've taken it to heart (pun intended). Keep up the good work during the time you have left.*
>
> *Please accept my very best wishes for a successful career in the Law. You've got what it takes to be an outstanding lawyer. I hope we see each other again soon.*
>
> *Timothy Goode*

"Nice letter," Gordon said. "Short and sweet."

"That's Goodie . . . short and sweet. The fewer words the better, and if you can't be positive, be quiet."

She gave Gordon a warm kiss and traipsed off to hang up her coat and change into workout togs.

"See you later, Darling," she hailed on her way through the living room. "Eight okay for dinner?"

"No problem. I ordered in tonight. It'll be here around then."

GEORGETOWN, MD

Gordon directed the taxi driver to let him out a couple of blocks from Joan Chatrier's home in Georgetown. No point making his presence too obvious. Guests arriving in taxis were high visibility, and there were many *in the know* people in this tight little community. He recalled the story of the Argentine ambassador stealing a visit with a Senator's wife, and being recognized by the neighbor across the street.

On the ten-minute ride from his office at 17th NW, he thought back to the moment Joan Chatrier had left the law firm he now managed for a practice more accommodating to her chosen specialty.

"I envy your new partners, Joan, and the reputation you're bringing to their practice," he told her. *"We'll miss your bright intellect around here."*

He walked now up the red brick steps, counting to six as he reached the level of her front door. He paused there before ringing the doorbell. He had a sense of having done this before . . . interviewing Joan on behalf of the White House staff, but he'd hardly known any of them the last time he stood in front of this door. He took a deep breath and rang the bell.

Chatrier came to the door in slacks and a sweater, looking more like a T.V. mom than a middle-aged candidate for the Supreme Court. The off-white turtleneck complimented the olive tone of her skin and accentuated a remarkable profile.

"Come in, Gordon," Joan said, adding as he stepped into the foyer, "I hope spring is early this year. I hate this cold weather."

"I agree." He shed his topcoat and folded it over an arm.

"When was the last time you were in my home, Gordon?" She opened the hall closet door and handed him a coat hanger.

"I'm not sure, Joan, but it looks as grand as I remember."

"Well, come on back," Joan Chatrier said. "Let's do this in the garden room. I've made it ready for the inquisition."

Today became yesterday for Gordon as they walked on hardwood floors over antique French throw rugs, through the front hall and back to the break between the kitchen and a small dining room. From there he followed as Joan angled right a few paces past the powder room and into a large wood paneled living area with high ceilings and full length French doors leading out to a brick patio and an English garden beyond. Facing the garden from the opposite side of the room was a large, lighted fireplace with numerous inlays and decorated with framed photographs from happier connubial times.

"That's a nice shot of you and Andre," he said, taking in the room at a glance.

Joan nodded. "There's a good one of the two of you back there on the other wall."

He walked to where Joan motioned with a swing of her hand as she took a seat at the card table she'd installed for the occasion. The photo was from around the time Joan and the Frenchman had met, the picture taken on the Eastern Shore of Maryland at a summer outing of his law firm. The older Andre Chatrier appeared as dashing as Gordon remembered him.

Another photo caught his eye. Framed among a grove of southern oaks with long strands of Spanish moss hanging from their branches, a tall woman and young child stood hand in hand, posed for the photographer. The woman's skin was ebony colored, and she was strikingly beautiful.

"She was something, wasn't she?" Joan said.

"That's your mother and you?"

She nodded. "A long time ago."

"New Orleans?"

"Ummm. That whole grove of trees was wiped out in a big hurricane."

"How's your mother doing?" he asked.

"She's the same. Calls me every day, worried that I don't have a regular job," she said, laughing with affection at her mother's preference.

"I guess the Supreme Court might qualify," he said.

"You know, it's funny, but I doubt it. I think Mother would be happier if I cleaned houses like she used to do."

"You're not serious."

"Close to it. When Andre died, I tried to get her to move here, but she'd have none of it. She was certain I'd soon be running back home."

"She and Andre get along okay?" he asked out of curiosity, making his way to the card table and chairs she'd arranged.

"Fine, considering no one was good enough for her daughter. And don't forget, she grew up in Martinique where aristocratic Frenchmen have some historical mischief to overcome. One of them was probably my father," she said, holding her hands palms-up to demonstrate the color contrast.

He considered the obvious question coming from that statement. Instead he asked, "Have you told her yet?"

"Nothing to tell, is there? Everything in its time and place."

"Shall we get to work then?" he said, taking his appointed seat. "Before we dive into the abyss, I have a thought for you."

Joan waited patiently with the slightest hint of a bemused smile.

"Be yourself," he said. "Don't try to be what you think a Supreme Court justice should be, and don't let me or anyone else try to change you."

"You sound just like my mother."

He laughed. "Are you ready for FBI agents poking into every corner of your life?" he asked, opening up the loose-leaf notebook he'd brought with him and placing a small tape recorder on the table between them.

"I don't have much choice, do I?"

"You'll find it an intrusive if very routine process. Of course, they're always looking for items that make them look thorough and you nefarious. So they get into personal stuff that has no relevance to the position you're being nominated to fill. They love to find a good sex angle. Got any of those?"

"Sex angles?"

"Any skeletons or bad boyfriends?"

"Don't I wish? I'm about as celibate as you'll find outside the nunnery. Maybe inside, as well."

He smiled at the touch of humor. "They'll go back through your whole adult life, Joan," he said, a hint of skepticism in his voice. Joan didn't appear to see it herself, but she was at least as attractive as her mother had been at her age. "So, if there's anything there, you ought to tell me about it."

"All my deviant behavior was accomplished before I was three."

He smiled again. "Anything else? False statements, unkempt friends, family trysts? You know the drill."

"I can't really think of anything noteworthy. I copied a friend's homework in sixth grade. I've had a few traffic tickets. And I played the one-arm bandits when I was in Las Vegas on the Red Dog case."

"Finances?"

"Andre left me comfortably well off. I've got a mortgage. It gives me a tax deduction."

"Speaking of taxes . . ."

"I have it done professionally. I report all my income and pay my taxes on time."

He turned a page in his notes. "You speak three languages, if I remember. Where'd you pick up Spanish?"

"I went to school in Puerto Rico, remember?"

"Of course. I forgot that. Anything there to talk about?"

"I had a part-time paying job, working for a group that pushed independence for Puerto Rico. That was big during the time I was there."

"What'd you do?"

"I helped edit their propaganda."

"Were you active in that cause?"

"Not really. I had some sympathy for their idealism, but remember my mother had emigrated from another Caribbean island. I knew Puerto Ricans were better off being part of the U.S."

He smiled at her ability to take on a potentially embarrassing disclosure like writing copy for the Puerto Rican independence movement, and make herself credible by referring to her mother's background in Martinique. Who would doubt she'd seen through their idealism?

"So you didn't march in rallies or throw rotten tomatoes?"

"I went to rallies. The food was free, and I wanted to see how the editing I'd done paid off. It was clinical, not political."

He thought that would pass muster, too.

As they continued through the list, Joan picked up more expression in her voice and seemed to enjoy the process.

"Okay, let's push some of the hot buttons," he said. "I'll give you a keyword. You tell me your very first impulse, then elaborate as you see fit."

"Shoot."

He led the way through the issues that most interested the President and her chief of staff, giving special attention also to those he thought would be the focus of the Senate Judiciary Committee—illegal immigration and the constitutional rights of persons who were not citizens, same sex marriage, *Roe v. Wade*, the new Patriot Act, ever-increasing government intrusion into the everyday lives of its citizens, and the competing roles of Congress and the executive branch under the Constitution. Joan's responses were animated and well thought out. They enjoyed the back and forth and time passed quickly. It was after eleven before they began to wind down.

"Do you know the retiring justice?" he asked.

"I've met him a few times. Why? Is that important?"

"Do you agree with his opinions?"

Joan paused and looked keenly at him, searching for motives in his question and glancing at the recorder blinking on the table. "Let me put it this way," she said after a few moments. "I probably wouldn't be Timothy Goode's choice for a replacement."

The clock in the hall sounded midnight as Joan finished responding to the last subject on the President's list.

"Will you walk back to the Watergate?" Joan asked. "I guess you can still get a cab down on 'M' or Wisconsin. How about a drink to warm you up?"

He nodded.

"Do you still use those awful gin martinis?"

CENTER STAGE

Charles Black was on the phone two days after Gordon turned in the list of issues and recorded responses from his session with Joan Chatrier.

"I think we can do this quickly," Charles said. " What do you think?"

"Whatever you want. I'm sure you've other equally important items on your agenda." He was delighted not to go over to the White House again, but this was not a particularly good omen for Chatrier.

"We've studied the transcript you provided us," Black said, "and listened to the tape. I must say, Gordon, you did a superb job . . . so even and reasonable that we can't tell if this woman is liberal or conservative. We expected Joan of Arc, but what we heard and read was more like Abraham Lincoln. Were you surprised by the answers she gave you?"

Gordon relaxed, and the tension left his muscles. "They're answers from on high."

"Explain, please."

"When Joan goes to court on behalf of one of her underdog clients, she's an advocate. She brings her six-foot frame, flashing dark eyes, sharp intellect, and an intensity to the defense of her client or the destruction of her opponents' position. She knows how to use her blackness, and her arguments are brilliant. She can mesmerize a jury. She might do that on the court, too, in an effort to bring others to her side, but what we asked her were big picture questions as they may come before the High Court. She answered, as the law professor she currently is, not as an advocate trying to persuade. Was I surprised? No. But whether her kind of persuasive energy, which you haven't yet seen, is what the President wants on the court, that's a different question. She'd become a force there, without question."

"We thought she might take the bit between her teeth more."

"If they only knew. And right all the nation's wrongs?" he said.

"Yes, like the things Joan of Arc might have thought were worth dying for."

The Joan of Arc reference, Gordon felt certain, had come directly from the President. "Joan's respectful of the process," he said, "but I'd assume, if I were you guys, that she'd be proactive as a judge."

"She *is* direct. No bullshit anywhere in her answers."

Gordon laughed. That remark could have come from the President, too. "You don't always get what you see, Charles. You'd better assume she will be a force on the court."

"That's okay, but I found it a bit strange that the City of New Orleans would bring in a pregnant woman to work as a maid."

He hadn't thought about that. "I agree with you, Charles. It's at least unusual. I guess they thought Joan's mother was an exceptional find. She spoke English as well as French. She was very attractive, too. Maybe that helped," he added, some cynicism in his voice.

"Yes, well, we haven't made up our minds yet."

"Take your time with this, Charles," he said, and then, in his usual lawyers sign off, said, "and let me know if you need anything more."

Gordon wondered, after hanging up the phone, whether his session with Joan had killed any chance she had to land the appointment. Maybe he'd done too good a job, allowing Joan to be very frank and bringing out her quick opinions on the issues. He wasn't even sure he wanted her to be the President's choice. He felt certain her true progressive bias would not come out until she got on the court. He had no doubt that the President saw in

Joan Chatrier the opportunity to add one-plus to the balance on the court. It was great politically for the President to be able to appoint a black woman whose mother had come in the country to work as a servant. It covered some of the President's priorities. But Gordon knew Joan. She'd be uncommonly persuasive, even within that confident assembly of bright minds up there on the Hill. He was also sure that he was not the only Washingtonian who would recognize Joan's talents at compelling progressive conclusions in others. As he'd told Charles, Joan would be a force on the court. That was going to cause some people to vote against her. The President might be the first, but when push came to shove, Gordon doubted that.

When Gordon, too, had finished showering, he joined Kate in the corner of the apartment that overlooked the Kennedy Center and the Potomac River toward Arlington. She was curled up in her favorite chair, reading the *Sunday Post*, and looked up as Gordon approached. His presence made the words in the *Post* come alive for her.

"You're right smack in the middle of presidential choice politics, Gordon."

"You think so?" he said with a wink.

She didn't want a wink. She wanted a serious discussion. "There's plenty of opposition. If this appointment turns out to be a disaster, where is the world going to look?"

Gordon nodded. "Disaster for me or the White House?"

"What's the difference?" she asked.

Gordon laughed, and nodded again. "Depends on the kind of disaster."

"Sure, but read today's paper," she said, holding it up. "Everyone on Capitol Hill thinks Joan Chatrier was your recommendation to the President. If you don't believe me, have a look."

He smiled, and took the paper from her outstretched hand.

"If she's the President's choice, I'll need to speak with the Chief Justice," she said. "Everyone I know is familiar with my significant other. If you're involved, I'm involved."

"Sorry about that."

"Hey, I like it that way. I'm not long for the clerkship, anyway."

"You go to my head, Kate Stevens," Gordon said, handing back the paper and moving over to the couch. "So tell me . . . what are the pundits advising the President?"

"The President has really surprised everyone with her short list. I think even you were surprised."

"She likes doing that."

"But has she made a mistake this time?"

"Is that what they're saying?"

"Some are. The Washington columnists seem especially worked up over Joan Chatrier's being one of the possibilities. She was not first on any Washington list. They don't know her views on anything."

"If she's selected, Joan will surprise them, and in the process the President will use the conflict to make all her points about the direction in which she expects to lead the country."

"So the two are connected at the hip . . . Joan's character and success on the court, and the President's popularity."

"Yes, she needs this appointment to go well from day one. It can do a lot of damage to her other programs if it doesn't."

"I don't see any of that reflected in the *Post*," she said.

"There's nothing Washington insiders despise more than being forced to accept someone they've never considered themselves. The media will go after Joan if she's the President's choice, and destroy her if she lets them. If the choice is Joan . . . Joan being Joan will bring the better journalists over to her side when they get that glimpse. It may take some doing for that to happen. Barring some major scandal, it'll probably all come down to her performance on television before the Senate Judiciary Committee. It's what she'll be like once she gets on the court that worries me."

Kate raised her eyebrows. "Won't that be too late? I mean, how likely is it the committee would not confirm her?"

"Not too likely, unless some unsavory connection turns up casting a shadow on the President's choice. The President has a lot at stake here. This is her first big court appointment. It will show a stunning weakness in her presidency if she loses. Remember Judge Robert Bork?" Gordon said.

"Before my time," she said with an actor's scowl. "But that's one out of how many?"

"There've been a few. Lyndon Johnson had a big problem when his appointee actually resigned after getting there. This President will feel she's lost the battle if her appointee doesn't come out of the Senate sessions as the clear choice for the nation, not just the presidential choice. She'd put her own credentials on the line by appointing Joan Chatrier."

Kate cocked her head to the side and squinted. "You can see here," she said pointing to the editorial page, "that the press has started to sift through her life with a magnifying glass. Be sure to read this article," she said, holding up a half page synopsis of Joan Chatrier's major cases and the large corporations and their lawyers that were lined up against her.

Gordon nodded. "If Joan handles that right she can emerge looking like a super hero, not a villain."

"And who is going to handle it right for her, you?"

He laughed. "No, not me. The White House PR gang is already at work on all three final candidates."

But she wanted to stay focused on Joan Chatrier. "Can Joan live up to the billing?"

"We'll see, Kate, I guess we'll see."

"What about the FBI investigation?"

"That's step two. The Department of Justice has already completed a pretty thorough search into the lives of all those candidates still on the President's short list."

"And found nothing on Joan?"

"I don't think it turned up much. Her mother comes from Martinique, and the people there are still friends of ours."

That sparked some recall in Kate's mind. "Even though they helped the Cuban revolutionaries?"

"Where'd you come up with that bit?"

It was unusual that she would remember something like this and Gordon wouldn't. "Don't you remember?"

"Can't say that I do," he said, shaking his head.

"I think it was you . . . it must have been you . . . who told me after one of your meetings when we were in Havana that Che Guevara and Fidel Castro met with a French government arms dealer in Martinique before they made the big push into Havana. Remember?"

"That sounds vaguely familiar, but I don't think Joan had anything to do with that. She hadn't even been born yet."

"That's not what I meant. I only mentioned it because you asked me where I came up with that bit of history," she said with measured annoyance in her tone.

"Oh, sorry, but I haven't got wind of any scandals. Joan says there aren't any, but you never know. There are always going to be a few surprises, with all the usual consequences."

THE OVAL OFFICE

Charles Black began his day, like most, together with the President in her office. Occasionally, others were present, but not on this day.

"Joan Chatrier is a dream come true for us," the President told her chief of staff when he relayed Gordon Cox's mild surprise at her choice, "and if Gordon didn't think she'd be a good addition to the court, he would have said so weeks ago."

Black's impression was that Gordon Cox had changed his view slightly after becoming involved in the selection process, but he'd chosen not to pursue the issue. "She'll be controversial, Madam President. You know that."

"I know, but it'll be worth every minute, Charles."

"Some will say she's too inexperienced, but a lot of them will just mean she's trouble."

"I know, I know, just bring'em on. But you and Gordon will have to work as a team on this, like you did in my campaign. You two were the magic."

This was no problem for Black. He liked working with Gordon. "When do you want to see her?" he asked.

"Let's have her come in later this week for a one on one. If I can get there with her, we'll make the appointment, and let the opposition in the Senate take their best shot."

"So it's a done deal?" Kate asked as she appeared from the den and watched Gordon hang his coat in the hall closet. He walked across the living room and gave her a hug.

"It looks that way," he said, "but the President's meeting with Joan next week."

"The news has certainly leaked out. Is that on purpose?"

"I think that came out of the Senate. Henry Minturn is still looking for enough media objections to convince the White House that Joan's not the right choice."

Kate moved toward the den. "Get comfortable, Honey, and I'll tell you the latest from Law Clerk Heaven."

"Okay, what'll it be, red or white?"

"I have a big glass of water on the desk. I'll stick with that for now. I drank too much at the shindig last night."

He knew that wasn't so, and he was going to have a drink even if she wasn't. "I'll join you in a couple of minutes," he said, disappearing into their bedroom to change out of his business suit.

When he joined her in the den, Kate leaned way back in her chair and announced, "The chief justice gave us four clerks at large our walking orders today."

"What's the timing?"

"In a minute. First, I have to tell you what he said to me. He held me back when the other three left, and brought up the subject of my old movie."

"Did he give it a good review?" Gordon laughed. This film was the catalyst that had brought Gordon and Kate together two years previously. It was Kate's law journal article on the constitutionality of the Cuban embargo, produced as a fictional film story good enough to be shown at a formal dinner in the White House.

"Very funny, but he was serious. He asked me whether anyone had called me about it."

Gordon's brow wrinkled, and he squinted at her.

"When I said no one had, he said to please tell him if they did. When I asked him why that was important, he said the court should not get involved in politics, especially when it related to a presidential appointee to the court, and that this included law clerks."

"I don't get it."

"He receives calls from time to time. He probably needs to be able to shake them off. If they knew one of the law clerks had taken some kind of political position, he might have difficulty doing that."

Gordon nodded and seemed to change the subject. "What did he say about your time left?"

"He asked us to stay on at least until the new justice has organized his or her office. There's no lack of things for us to do."

"So, what are your plans?"

"Have you looked at the mail on the hall table?"

Gordon had seen the letters coming in from D.C. law firms. "Take your time with that, Katie. There's no rush."

"All four of us are getting barraged. Why do you think I haven't opened any of them?"

He nodded appreciation for that small favor. He didn't need this kind of distraction with the Chatrier appointment heating up. Getting into private practice was one of the most important things that would ever happen in Kate's life, but it was not going to be easy for him either. When Kate began working with another Washington law firm, he feared it would change their relationship. They'd talked it over, and decided that husband and wife or affianced lawyers should not be in the same firm. That was fine in theory, but Gordon wasn't so sure, now that the moment was at hand, that he wanted to share Kate with one of his competitors.

Kate noticed his distraction. "A penny for your thoughts."

"They're not worth a penny," he said, trying, but not completely managing, a smile.

"I'm going to take it slow, Gordon. Installation of a new justice has to be months away. Confirmation alone will take us into June, won't it?"

"I should think so."

"So I have time. As you said, there's no rush."

One politician's dream is another's nightmare. Senator Henry Minturn was running into opposition from within his own party as the word on the President's choice filtered through the Senate. On the other side of the aisle, all hell was breaking loose.

"We got to stop this appointment, Senator. I've been up all night with pictures of that woman dressed in a black robe, sitting up there on the bench and lecturing me on the rights of whistle blowers and hypocrites. Where in hell did the White House come up with this one? Who's pushing her?"

"I have my staff digging into her background. Nothing yet, but we'll come up with something, and take it from there."

"Can't we get her untracked before she's announced? I'll ask you again, who's really behind this selection? If she's a flaming do-gooder, it'll undo everything we've accomplished over the past twenty years."

"We don't know enough about her yet. Don't jump to conclusions. Sometimes, you know, the judges we pick turn out very different once they get on the court."

"I'll give you that, but I have a bad feeling about this one."

"The word is she'll announce the appointment week after next. We're caucusing on Friday. I'll try to pull something together by then."

Charles Black escorted the prospective Supreme Court appointee into the Oval Office. Joan appeared striking in a gray pinstriped pants suit that flowed with her as she entered the room. Not for a second did she relinquish eye contact with the President. Rebecca met her half way across the room in her usual fashion, a hand outstretched. They moved together around the office like two ballerinas in a solo-sex pas de deux.

"Thank you for accommodating our schedule, Joan. You look very judicial," the President said, glancing at her chief of staff. "Doesn't she, Charles?"

"Thank you, Madam President," Joan Chatrier said as Black nodded his agreement. "It's an honor for me to be here."

The President smiled as they stood in the center of the oval. "You're my choice, Joan. So you'd better tell me now whether there are any good reasons I shouldn't put you on the court. You may tell me while I'm searching your soul."

Joan lowered her head as the President focused sharply on her. "I'm pretty much what-you-see-is-what-you-get, Madam President. But I'm happy to address any questions or issues you have."

The President thought Joan Chatrier was anything but what you saw. She nodded to Charles, who shut the door on his way out. Then, she motioned for Joan to take a seat next to the large coffee table at one side of the room, and she sat across from her guest.

The two women talked for the better part of an hour, the President asking most of the questions and Joan responding. In the process, they explored views on the U.S. Constitution, the federal system that it created, and national issues social and antisocial in nature.

"The way I see this, Joan, is that you're too good to be true. I'm using you . . . I'm sure you realize that . . . to show that we can be what we choose to be when we're pointed in the right direction. Your mother must be someone very special."

Joan beamed. "She is, Madam President. She certainly is."

The President smiled. "I want your success to go 'round the world.' Can you carry such a burden, Joan Chatrier?"

"It won't be a completely new experience, Madam President."

The President smiled. Joan's reply had hit the mark. She knew what the President expected, and would have no silly self-doubts or emotions getting in her way. "Okay, good," the President said. "We'll make the announcement next Tuesday. Are you available?"

Charles Black had tipped Joan on the date. "Absolutely."

"Good, then it's done." The President paused, as if forgetting something. Then, she asked, "Don't you have any questions for me?"

The candidate clasped her hands as if to begin a prayer. "I might ask you, Madam President, what you see as the most important issues that are likely to come before the court over the next decade."

The President was disappointed by Joan's soft pitch. She'd expected something more challenging, but answered with as much passion as she could summon. "Oh, my goodness, I have no crystal ball, but they're already here, I think. We need to decide what kind of a world we want to live in, and how to make liberty work better. We're so fortunate to have a Constitution that bends and doesn't break. But we need people on the court to have a vision and a set of principles to see us through the global challenges coming our way. It's people who know an issue when they see it that I want to add to the court. I don't want the issues to define us."

The politics involved in the Senate confirmation of Joan Chatrier to the Supreme Court began to heat up by arithmetic progression as warm weather crept tentatively into the nation's capitol. By the following week, Joan Chatrier was on everyone's front page. Those who would not have a plaintiff's lawyer on the court, or one so young, manned their bulldozers and began to scrape for dirt.

Senator Henry Minturn gave them plenty of time to do their work. He scheduled the confirmation hearing before the Senate Judiciary Committee for four weeks after Congress's Easter recess.

THE SENATE

It was snowing lightly when Kate's alarm went off at 6 a.m. Gordon was already frying up eggs in the kitchen. The smell of freshly brewed coffee and sizzling bacon got her quickly out of bed and into the shower. She let the warm water splash on her forehead, run through her fine blond hair, and down the slender curves of her body. She looked through the shower door, and watched flakes of snow float by the window, reflecting light from the street below.

Gordon knocked on the bathroom door as she stepped out of the shower. "Come on in," she said, using a towel around her waist as an immodest robe.

Gordon greeted her with a low whistle. "Your breakfast is ready, Beautiful. I've agreed to be over at the White House in thirty minutes."

"Our favorite President?" she asked, slipping her arms into the sleeves of her bathrobe and tying the belt around her middle.

"Charles Black and the chairman of the Senate Judiciary Committee."

"On Joan Chatrier?"

"The one and only," he said.

"Charles is calling in his chips," she said, seeing Gordon's involvement for what it was . . . backing up the White House.

She'd already guessed from what Gordon had told her that Charles Black might have preferred Chatrier to have received less help navigating the vetting process. Chatrier certainly gave Charles the biggest challenge of all those they'd considered. So, Gordon got me here . . . let him take some of the heat.

"See, I told you," Kate said. "You're linked to that appointment for now and forever."

Gordon laughed. "How come you're so smart?"

She gave Gordon a squeeze and a long, deep kiss. Then, she headed for the kitchen.

Kate liked walking in the falling snowflakes. Washington's weather for nine months was erratic. The other three it was just plain stifling hot. The wet snow would turn to rain later, but, in the early morning, it was still light and fluffy, and she reveled in it. She had the streets and parks on her long walk almost to herself. Even the cordoned off area around the White House appeared void of its usual sparse crowds. The lights were on in the office building where she knew Gordon was meeting with the President's chief of staff and the formidable and grumpy Senator Minturn. She wondered what they were saying at that moment.

Her thoughts shifted to a case she'd be working on that day. It was easy to connect the two events because they both involved the Supreme Court. It was going to be fun to see how all that lay ahead would play out: getting Joan Chatrier confirmed, seeing how she integrated with the other justices, and how the President's popularity would suffer or gain in the process. Kate had a ringside seat for the big game of constitutional democracy in action. As always, it excited her.

What was less exciting were the strange looks coming her way from the senior law clerk for the chief justice. When she couldn't stand it any longer she confronted him. It caught him off guard.

"George, is something troubling you? You seem to have something on your mind."

"What, oh, no, why do you ask?"

"Well, for starters, you look at me like I'm one of the terrorists."

"What? I'm sorry . . ." He looked at her with his head cocked to one side, finding courage to speak. "I saw the film you produced when you were at Georgetown. It was well done . . . very professional."

She hesitated. "Did the chief ask you to watch it?"

He peered at her again from a side view. "Er, ah, yes, actually, he did."

"Didn't you ever write a law review note when you were at school?"

"Of course."

"Well, that's what that was . . . in a form that I hoped more people would have the opportunity to see than words squirreled away in the *Georgetown Law Journal.*"

He nodded an appreciation for the point she made, and they let it drop. It still worried Kate, but at least he wasn't giving her the fisheye any longer.

"It's a comfort knowing who your friends are," Charles Black said, passing a plate of assorted doughnuts to Gordon Cox and Henry Minturn, chairman of the Senate Judiciary Committee, as they sat at the small, round table in the center of Black's large conference room.

"And your enemies." Minturn said, peering over at Gordon and leaning forward until his ample stomach folded over the table's edge. He carefully selected one covered with chocolate. Then, as if expressing guilt for his first choice, he added a plain cruller. He placed both on the plate next to his coffee cup, straightened up, and continued speaking. "Is it that she hates me, Charles, or just that she likes a good fight? Getting this progressive plaintiff's lawyer, all due respect to you, Mr. Cox, through confirmation is going to take divine intervention. What in God's good name was she thinking?"

Black took an embarrassed glance at Gordon, and said to Minturn, "Gordon's not a progressive, Henry."

The senator did not look at Gordon when he answered, "Maybe not, but his pretty, young girlfriend is. Didn't you ever see her film on Cuba?"

Gordon laughed. "I think you better explain that remark, Senator. We've all seen that film, and unless you don't remember that pretty, young woman, as you call her, almost lost her life on a mission to Cuba on behalf of our President, trying along with me to fix some of the foreign policy sinkholes you and your colleagues in Congress have led us into over the past sixty years."

Charles Black raised both his hands, touchdown style, as Gordon eased back into his seat. "Enough, my friends. This will not get us anywhere."

"I think we should know what brought this on, Charles," Gordon said. "Why, all of a sudden, is Kate's three-year-old film so important?"

Minturn saw that as his cue. "Okay, I'll tell you why . . . because my colleague from Illinois thinks your girlfriend . . . or whatever she is to you . . . was involved in a conspiracy with a young journalist working for the *International Herald Tribune* . . . a conspiracy that got the journalist killed. The Chicago police are looking into it, and they've already questioned your Ms. Stevens for her involvement. We think maybe the French newspaper asked this journalist to look into the effects of the Cuban embargo on the country and he hooked up with his old friend, Katherine. You, Sir, were apparently not her first male companion."

Gordon was still focused on the Chicago police questioning Kate. *Kate had mentioned it, but this sounded more serious.*

"This woman, Chatrier, that the President has now appointed also made it clear that she'd hold the Cuban embargo unconstitutional. If you don't see a connection here, I sure as hell do."

Gordon started to reply, but Charles held up a hand. "Henry, you know damn well the President never liked that embargo. It helped keep those sons-a-bitches in power for over sixty years. She's certainly not going to appoint someone who doesn't agree with her."

Minturn snorted as loud as Black had ever heard him, but he raised the palms of his hands in surrender . . . for the moment, at least.

Black picked up where he'd left off. "Chatrier's a good choice, Henry. What's the vote look like?"

"What vote? If we put it on the floor today, I told you . . . she wouldn't get forty yeas."

"What are the main objections?"

"You want the real reasons, or what they are going to say?"

"Only what's fit to print, Henry," said Charles Black, taking another glance at Gordon.

"Too aggressive, inexperienced as a judge, way too minority oriented, and a manipulator of the law to her own purposes. As unfit to judge as the last president was to lead the nation. Besides, who really knows anything about her?"

Black coughed. "We'll know her pretty darn well before this thing is over, I reckon."

"You really think so? My bet is you won't know squat until you see her in action on the court. So appoint the woman to the Civil Rights Commission, not the Supreme Court. Charles, I got to tell you, there's something about this woman . . . I can't put my finger on it, but she scares me."

Realizing that Gordon was not immediately coming to his aid, Black took up the cause for Joan Chatrier. "Name a better candidate for the court," he countered. "We think she matches up well with all those on the list your committee was given."

Minturn snorted . . . not so loud this time. "That's not saying a hell of a lot. You could have put her on a Court of Appeals for a few years, maybe then to the High Court if she doesn't turn out to be a legal subversive."

Charles Black shifted in his chair and looked at Gordon. "The President wants her on there now. So let's get moving on this."

"What's he doing here anyway?" Minturn asked, snorting and pointing his thumb in the direction of Gordon.

Black reddened, showing embarrassment for Gordon, who continued to ignore the senator's attempt at a put down.

"He knows Joan as well as anyone," Black said. "We thought you might want to ask him some questions."

Minturn took a large bite of the donut in his hand, turned, and looked squarely at Cox. With his mouth half full, he managed, "She was your boss at the law firm?" he mumbled through the dough.

"We were at the same firm, Senator. She's older, yes, and a litigator."

"So she wasn't your boss?"

"No, indeed, she was not."

"But she was your recommendation to the President."

Gordon smiled, showing teeth and exchanging another glance with Charles Black. "Neither the President nor Charles asked me for any recommendations, Senator. The President did ask a few pointed questions about this appointee, for which I was happy to find some answers. I'm pleased to do the same for you."

Henry Minturn snorted and asked Cox, "So what are the skeletons in her closet?"

"None of which I'm aware, Senator."

"Is that what you told the FBI when they came calling?"

"They didn't ask me that question specifically. But they did seem interested in skeletons, mostly of the sexual kind, along with her client base. I wasn't much help in that area, but she has no deviant tendencies current or past, as far as I know. The bureau is being quite thorough in interviewing her acquaintances on social behavioral patterns."

"We don't have the *special investigation report* yet, but she's an attractive woman and single. She must have men chasing her all over town. I guess, if there are any red flags in there, we'll know about it pretty quick. What about her political leanings? Is she Muslim or anything like that?"

"She and her husband were married in the Methodist church right here in the district. That I know, because I was there."

"How far out left is she?"

"She shares much of the President's values, Senator . . . maybe a bit more liberal, I guess you could say."

"Meaning she's way left of you. And you, maybe, are a bit right of me?"

"Something like that."

"Abortion?"

"She'd look at *Roe v. Wade* as a controlling judicial precedent."

"Bussing school kids, affirmative action, immigration?"

"On the liberal side, I would say, but no zealot."

"Tort reform?"

"Perhaps, but remember, she's a plaintiff's lawyer."

"The Electoral College Amendment?"

"I honestly don't know. You'd have to ask her."

"Statehood for Puerto Rico?"

That seemed an odd question coming from a leading Senator at this point. This wasn't a hot button anymore. Instead of asking why that might be important, as he wanted to, Gordon used what Joan had told him when asked a similar question. "I doubt she'd have strong feelings one way or the other, but if push came to shove, my guess is she'd be against independence for Puerto Rico based on her mother's experience coming from Martinique."

"I heard she used to travel to Cuba from San Juan. Know anything about that?"

"Who told you that?" Charles Black interrupted.

"I dunno. It's circulating around because of that article she wrote," the senator said, and looking back to Gordon, he asked, "Did her mother get married here?"

"No. I believe she was pregnant with Joan when she arrived."

"So Chatrier's native born."

"That's my understanding."

"Treatment of illegal aliens? What's her position on educating and doctoring their children?"

"I'd be guessing, Senator, but Joan has always reasoned things out. She's basically free of extreme bias and prejudice, but she likes doing battle for the underdog."

"I guess she has that in common with our President," Minturn said. Turning to address Charles Black, he continued in a different vein, "We'll do the best we can, Charles. No promises, and you better have someone check out this connection with Cuba. It's going to bring you all down if you're not careful. There're still a lot of your constituents who think the Castros were communists thugs. And you better warn the President, Charles, this will be one hell of a battle. She'd best be ready to make some deals. I guess we're going to find where her real priorities are."

Black gave Gordon their code *finger across the nose* to please stick around as Minturn prepared to leave the meeting.

After Charles was sure the senator was out of hearing, he sat down and looked at Gordon. "Phew, he's always a challenge, that man. So what's all this stuff about Kate, Gordon?"

"She *was* interviewed by the Chicago police . . . not questioned. The boy who was killed and Kate were in the same study group first year at Georgetown. Good friends, probably more than that if the truth be known, but if Kate were involved in some joint exercise with him, I'd know about it. Hells bells, where would she get the time?"

"This guy was killed out in Chicago?"

"Apparently Kate received a call from the man's mother a couple of days ago. It really upset her. The mother hates her. I think Kate helped her son escape parental control at the start of their second year at law school, and the mother thinks she was involved in his going to Chicago, where he was killed. I'm sorry, Charles, but that's about all I know."

"Okay. The good Senator Minturn loves to have something to throw at people he's meeting. This, I guess, was his fastball aimed at your head. I must say, you tolerated it well. I wanted to hit him."

Gordon laughed. "I'll speak about it with Kate tonight. If there's anything more you or the President should know, I'll give you a call."

"That's fine with me, Gordon. We'll be talking very soon in any case."

ADVISE AND CONFIRM

"I have Charles Black on the phone for you, Gordon," Emily said. She stood in the doorway to his office as she usually did when a call came in from the White House. The less others might hear from this source, the better, and she didn't use the intercom.

"You called?" Black asked.

"Yes, Charles. Kate and I talked about the Arnold case last evening. It looks like the good senator from Illinois is not letting this business drop. He's contacted the chief justice. Something like, '*What kind of people are you hiring for law clerks these days?*'" Kate was called in and asked about it yesterday afternoon. This, together with the movie she made three years ago on the Cuban embargo, has put her under a lot of pressure in chambers. Since her Justice Goode is not there anymore to battle for her, she thinks the chief justice may ask her to leave."

"I'm sorry to hear that, Gordon. Anything you want me to do?"

"Goodness, no. Neither Kate nor I want this to cause problems for you or the White House. This is Kate's battle, and I have no doubt she'll manage that just fine."

"Okay, but the offer stands. Now, I've got a favor to ask. The President would like you to get Chatrier up to speed. Give her some guidance for

69

handling the upcoming confirmation hearing before the Senate. What'd you lawyers call it . . . wood-shedding?"

Of course he'd do it. "She'll love that," he said with a laugh.

"Old Charlie Detwiler is going to walk her around the Senate office buildings next week. Could you do it before then?"

"I'll give her a call," he said.

"Thanks, Gordon, and find out if she's gotten any calls or threats about this Cuban business. It's looming as a big issue in Congress, and we'd like to nip it in the bud."

He wasted no time in corralling Joan for the upcoming confirmation hearing. Joan was attending a conference of law school professors in New York, and he decided an obscure hotel in mid-town Manhattan would be a good place to hold the session. Once there, they conducted a dress rehearsal of her appearance before the Senate Judiciary Committee.

"I've got the FBI traipsing around in my life now, Gordon. An agent insinuated Andre cheated on me during our marriage and that I cheated on him, as well. According to unidentified 'friends,' he and I visited group sex clubs, and, after his death, I became addicted to gambling and went to Las Vegas to indulge myself. I'm accused of driving to Atlantic City and registering under false names. I asked them who told them all this. You know the standard answer. They offered no proof of any of it because, of course, it's all untrue."

"They must have some evidence for the trips to Vegas. You can't make that up."

"Of course, I handled a case out there, remember? Two cases, actually."

"I remember 'Red Dog' and his tribe."

"Yes, and we accomplished a good settlement in that case. Half the land the State of Nevada did not reclaim, and damages for what they covered under 500 feet of water. In all, I probably went to Vegas a dozen or more times over a two or three year period. Andre came along to keep me company a couple of times." Joan stopped for a moment, took a tissue from her purse, and blew her nose. "God, I miss him, Gordon. I really do," she said, trying to smile, but not pulling it off.

They sat in silence, Gordon not wishing to interrupt a private moment as Joan pulled herself together.

"You asked me once whether I could handle the rarified air up there. You hit that nail on the head. That's what I fear most, being isolated on the mountain for the rest of my life. Maybe I'm too young for this job. I'm a trial lawyer, and I used to be a damn good one. How am I going to breathe up there, so far above the fray?"

Gordon had been waiting for this issue to come up. He'd been surprised she'd dismissed it so easily before. "Joan, you are going to be right smack in the middle of some of the broadest and most far-reaching decisions ever considered by Western Civilization. You'll be given the chance to strengthen our Constitution, and the way of life it has maintained. It will make the opportunities up to now seem almost incidental. And you are not too young. The chief justice is only a few years older. The President wants others who will be there long enough to provide continuity and stability over a time she believes the court will come under severe pressure to sway with the political winds."

Joan nodded several times, noting some acceptance to what he said, but she didn't seem convinced. "What would happen if I bailed out?"

He realized that adding more pressure by telling her she couldn't do that now would be counterproductive. "There'd be some embarrassment, but that could be managed, Joan. What would your mother think? I'd concentrate on that." As he spoke, he thought about what Charles Black had asked. "One more thing, Joan, have you been getting any calls or questions concerning the article you published several years ago on the Cuban embargo?"

"Only in class at GW."

"No harassing mumbo-jumbo?"

"No."

When they'd finished walking through the likely happenings before the Senate Committee, Gordon paid the front desk for the conference room, and they walked out through the lobby together.

"So you've finally met the right woman," Joan said. "I'm happy for you, Gordon. How does she like it over on the Constitution side of the Hill?"

"She wants to get started trying cases. Sound familiar?"

"Good for her. I only saw her for a few minutes at your engagement party. You're a dirty old man, Gordon Cox. She could be your baby sister if she weren't so good looking."

He laughed, but saw truth in Joan's statement. "Look who's talking. How old was Andre when you two got married?"

"Touché, Gordon, not much different, and I never had a moment of unhappiness with him. I wish he were going to be there when I come home from court every day. I wonder how the President does it. That's a big White House for a single woman to be rambling around in."

"I know. She joked the other day when we were talking about your upcoming confirmation hearing, that, while we're at it, maybe she should have the Senate confirm a live-in for her."

Chatrier laughed. "At one point, I thought she was going to adopt you."

"The live-in son of the President of the United States? Wow, that's getting up in the world. Anything you wish me to report to your President?"

Joan hunched her shoulders.

He nodded and played his last card. "I need to ask you one more time: is there anything we should know that we don't know? Any skeletons in the closet?" As he said those words he recalled the issue Senator Minturn had raised. "Henry Minturn mentioned something about your going to Cuba during the time it was very illegal to do that. He's getting banged on by somebody."

Joan looked surprised, and then smiled. "I wanted to go to Havana one time, but Mama raised hell about it. 'No daughter of mine is going to visit those pirates,'" she said, "or something like that. I don't know why she was so upset with the notion, but I never went."

He nodded. "That reminds me. How's your mother taking all the excitement?" he asked as the doorman produced a taxi and opened the door for Joan.

Joan sat on the corner of the car seat, one foot still on the curb. "She takes everything in stride, Gordon. I know she'll sit glued to the television screen during the Senate hearings. It'll be her Super Bowl." Chatrier's expression broke into a slight smile. She drew a deep breath, and told Cox, "I owe everything I have to her. She devoted her entire life to bettering mine. I wish I could get her to move to Washington. I won't have as much time for her as a Supreme Court justice. It's a worry I have, but not her. Anyway, she'll never move, so it's an academic point. Thanks for asking," she said, giving him a wave as she closed the cab door.

Gordon walked to Penn Station. He had a meeting in Wilmington, Delaware, and the Amtrak train was the quickest and most convenient way for him to travel back to the Potomac.

Landfills and sooty marshes rolled by Gordon's window as the best train in the country emerged from the Hudson River Tunnel and began its transit of New Jersey. His thoughts shifted from saltwater marshes to the President's appointment as the rails flew by under the highways leading south and west. He mulled over the session with Joan as the train stopped to pick up passengers at the New Jersey Amtrak station.

One of the boarding passengers waved to him from the platform. Gordon recognized Bradley Smyth, the lawyer who would attend the President's opposition at the Senate hearings on Joan's confirmation. Smyth waved again, and Gordon watched as he came onboard and marched in a straight line to where he sat.

"Good day, Gordon, may I join you?"

"Of course, Brad, let me move my case."

Smyth placed his own briefcase and coat on the empty seat across the aisle as the train pulled out of its stop in New Jersey. "I'll just bother you for a moment," he said, taking the seat next to Gordon and shaking his hand. "I was going to call you when I got to Washington. Can we chat?"

Gordon looked around to see if others were within earshot.

"We can speak quietly," Smyth said, seeing his discomfort. "We'll leave the shouting for our friends on the committee."

Gordon laughed. "On your way to the Hill?"

Smyth nodded, and with a smile that Gordon thought was forced, took a sheet of paper from the slim case he held on his lap. He handed it to Gordon. "Have a look at this," he said.

He unfolded crumpled, glossy paper. ASK HER WHO HER FA-THER IS was printed in large letters. The only address was TO THE SENATE JUDICIARY COMMITTEE.

"No signature or date, but as you can see," Smyth said, "it's on the back of a flyer, expounding in French the vacation pleasures of Martinique."

"Where'd you get this?" he asked.

"It was dropped off at the Senate office building and placed in Senator Brown's pigeon hole."

He looked over the note, folded it, and returned it to Smyth. "Interesting," he said, "and also irrelevant."

"I suppose so, but I have to ask you . . . "

"Brad, even if I knew anything about it, I wouldn't comment."

"The FBI doesn't have this letter," Smyth said.

Gordon looked out the window for a moment, watching the spires of Princeton University slide by in the distance. He turned back to the lawyer. "If that's the best those who wish her ill can do, I guess she'll be in good shape." He felt certain that Smyth had more on his agenda.

It took only another moment for Smyth to oblige. "Gordon, we took a look at the papers Joan filed when she applied for admission to the D.C. Bar. There's a discrepancy of at least a year, maybe two, in the chronology of her school and pre-school records. It's probably a simple error, but it's one of those things the committee can get pretty excited about."

"That's confidential information. How did you get your hands on that file?"

"You're right, and I can't tell you how I managed that feat. It's a good source because there's so much incentive to tell all when you're young. When you haven't had time to do much, and you're applying for admission to the Bar."

"I understand, but it's off limits," Gordon reminded him.

Smyth grimaced in a way that looked faked. "I know, but I need to be convinced it was a simple mistake that everyone missed, everyone including Joan Chatrier."

"Of course, it's an honest mistake. What would have been the point, to hide two years in first grade?"

"I agree, but that's what makes it interesting. And why didn't anybody pick it up?"

Smyth's last words on the subject kept coming back to Gordon later that day. He walked past Emily's vacant desk and opened the locked door into his office at the firm. "Maybe she still has her copy of that file," Smyth had said to him, suggesting Gordon might want to find out. "I know I kept mine. You could ask her to check the chronology, and that would be the end of it. You might be doing her a big favor."

He made the call.

"I don't have it, Gordon. Goodness no, I wouldn't keep stuff like that. Who told you this?"

"I can't tell you, Joan. I was hoping you had the file, that's all."

"Well, I don't."

He was surprised by what seemed a curt reply. He guessed Joan was not having a good day.

THE SENATE JUDICIARY COMMITTEE

Joan Chatrier's confirmation hearing got underway on a Tuesday morning with a touch of spring in the air. Those with the credentials, relationships, or the luck necessary to gain admission to the hearing room sat in rows of hardback chairs, which squeaked as those who occupied them moved and twitched while they waited for the star of the proceedings to arrive.

The President's choice took her place alone at a long table surrounded by microphones. She faced the huge half-moon shaped dais, behind which were placed the chairs for the nineteen senators who made up the Judiciary Committee, with the more senior senators near the middle and the junior rankings at either end. In back of each senator were places for staff members armed with notes and nudges to keep their boss up to speed with the proceedings and on track to say what they'd spent weeks rehearsing. As the hearing proceeded, some senators seemed to need more help than others. Not all the senators were present at all times, and some straggled in and out from time to time, which somehow gave a less than formal, almost rude, atmosphere to the work at hand.

The television cameras were well-placed to capture the drama. A limited number of other media types were discretely placed under the tall dais with their backs against its paneling and at the sides, alongside the gallery.

The television production resembled coverage of a major sporting event like Wimbledon or the World Series, including an analysis of the odds for or against confirmation. Joan was right . . . this would be her mother's Super Bowl.

Joan's above average height, erect posture, brilliant black hair flowing off her shoulders, flashing bright eyes, and perfect olive complexion gave an incandescent, surreal atmosphere to the proceedings. She faced the senators and cameras, and she could hear the movement of those seated at her back.

"Think of the group behind you as your support," Gordon had suggested. "Most of them will be on your side. You've been cast in the role of an underdog. America loves to side with the underdog."

Senator Henry Minturn, chairman of the committee, spent the better part of an hour outlining the procedural rules. The T.V. cable news stations used part of that time to go through, in dramatic fashion, the chronology of Joan's rise from a poor beginning in New Orleans to her prominence as one of the most successful trial lawyers in the country. Members of both political parties gave on-air interviews. They were given the opportunity to prejudge her case and to insert their own views on the function of the Supreme Court. These ranged from the court being a proactive politicized body to an appeal of last resort, limited to making decisions within the confines of the case before it. Such was the scope of the staged world within which the confirmation would be granted or denied.

The senator given the first questioning session after all the prelims and following a midday recess was a long-time and senior member of the Committee. He used a good portion of his allotted time to put forth a detailed but uninspired version of where the nation's judiciary stood and what the future held in store for the Supreme Court. It didn't sound to Joan like he thought she was any part of his solution. He wasn't very fond of lawyers like Joan Chatrier, whose livelihood involved being paid large sums for out-of-court decisions in their plaintiff client's favor.

After what seemed an unnecessarily long time, the senator peered down at Joan over his reading glasses and nodded to the chair that he was ready to begin asking his questions. The gallery hushed in anticipation because this man from the President's own political party was one of those who'd been less than enthusiastic in his support of Joan's appointment.

"Ms. Chatrier, if I may say so, you have most impressive credentials. If this government or some large corporation were stomping on my rights, I would most certainly want you in my corner. I'm a lawyer myself, and I've tried more than a few cases in my time . . . as counsel for the defense, of course, but none so noteworthy as the cases you've handled."

Joan Chatrier's first words, and the clear way in which she enunciated each syllable, were not lost on the assembled gallery. You could almost feel the level of interest rise up in anticipation of things to come.

"Thank you, Senator," Joan said. "I'm sure you're being too modest."

"Don't mention it, Counselor. We're all made or broken by our reputations, and yours as a trial lawyer is indeed remarkable."

Joan took his flattery as a precondition for what he had to say. *And now he's going to show you how smart he is, so look out.* Gordon's advice came through to her.

The senator paused, ostensibly to take a sip of water, but for those who knew him, for more dramatic effect in what followed. "What I want to know today is what makes you think this talent you so clearly have qualifies you to sit on the Supreme Court of the United States?"

Heeding Gordon's advice Joan paused before answering. "Most cases coming before the court were in the hands of trial lawyers at some point, Senator. Isn't that important?"

"That's what I'm asking you, Ms. Chatrier. Is that important, and if so, why? Is it because plaintiff's lawyers never say what they mean?" His comment aroused some rumbling from the gallery, but the senator was performing for some corporate and insurance clients of his own, and for a jury of television viewers. "Or is it that you, having been there, can determine what honest testimony is and what, on the other hand, is aimed to prejudice the simple-minded folks on the jury?"

Joan stifled her litigator's quick response, and took a long breath. "Senator, I may be missing your point, but I think it's much simpler than that.

I've heard it said that all politics are local. I think all appeals are local, too. What goes up on appeal can only be from what starts at trial. If you're on familiar ground in the trial court, you cannot be misled by grand sounding words in briefs or in oral statements before the court. You know how the facts were developed, and you know how and why the case came to the court. No trial lawyer could miss any of these essentials."

"Well . . ."

"Oh, and I don't think juries are simple-minded," she said, raising a muffled round of laughter from the audience.

The President, watching the television opening for a few minutes, thought to herself . . . *by God, maybe she is Joan of Arc.*

"Please," announced Henry Minturn from the committee chair, "don't make me clear the room." After assessing that his warning had been regarded, he said, "Proceed, Senator, you have three minutes remaining."

"Thank you, Mr. Chairman . . ." He directed his attention back to Joan. "Ms. Chatrier, have you ever sat on the bench . . . the bench of any court?"

"No, Senator, I have not."

The chairs in the room squeaked, and the chair raised his right hand in another warning.

"Do you know the age of the jurists presently on the Supreme Court?"

"I'm sorry, Senator, I do not."

"Hmm, would you care to know?"

Gordon Cox, watching at that moment on television, saw the trap being set. He hoped Joan recalled what they'd talked about. Asked such a question in private, Joan might follow her natural aggressiveness. "No, but I'm sure you're going to tell me." If she did that or, conversely, answered defensively, "They may have a couple of years on me," the senator could make her look naïve to his fellow senators on the dais and more importantly to those watching on television.

Instead, Joan said quietly, "I would care, senator," parrying the question and leaving him to carry his own ball across the line.

The senator tried again. "Do you have any idea, Ms. Chatrier, why most of those this senate has confirmed to the court were older than you?"

"No, Senator, I do not."

A few snickers sounded from the back of the room.

The senator looked dramatically over his reading specs. "Do you expect this panel to believe that?"

"I hope *you* believe me, Senator."

The back and forth went on for another minute before the chairman called for another recess. The general perception among those watching in the hearing room and on television: at the conclusion of her first testimony, the appointee had given as good as she'd had to take.

Joan was surprised that the senator hadn't gone into her childhood in New Orleans. The family for whom her mother had kept house in those days was well situated and politically powerful. It would have been polite for him to obtain their consent before bringing up the connection. Perhaps the family had said, "Please, don't."

THE ARROGANCE OF POWER

A senior senator from a large eastern state on a big river arrived the following morning with a toothy smile and an ingratiating nod to his imagined audience in the television gallery. He rushed to his place on the dais only moments before his turn came to question the appointee.

"Ms. Chatrier, hello, how are you this morning?" he asked with a cynical, pasted-on smile while sorting through the papers in front of him.

"I'm quite well, Senator. Thank you for asking."

"Yes, well, I for one am pleased our President has nominated someone to fill this High Court vacancy who can look at our constitution from a refreshing point of view, a view that has been missing in many judges for as long as I have been a member of this august body."

Joan squirmed a bit in her seat. Gordon Cox had warned her not to be complacent when those more or less on the same side of the aisle as the President began to compliment her.

"The thing you've got to worry about here," Gordon had told her, "is letting them put words into your mouth that the press and others not of like mind can pick up on later. Let them show off for the television cameras, but make them tow the line—your line—and do it politely as always. And look out for the Senator from the Empire State; he had his own recommendation to the President, and it wasn't you."

The senator continued. "You were born in Louisiana, if my notes are correct, Ms. Chatrier."

It was a question, and Joan answered it. "Yes, I was, Senator."

"Your mother came to this country to work in the household of a member of the House of Representatives, one of the grand old families of the South, I believe."

There, the cat was out of that bag. She wondered if the senator had made a deal with his colleague from Louisiana. "That's what I've been told, Senator," she said with a smile.

"Did your mother come in . . . do you know . . . on a valid visa to work here?"

"I believe so, yes."

"And if she did not, you'd still be a United States citizen."

"I would, Senator."

"Because you were born here?"

"That's right."

"Were you born here, Ms. Chatrier?"

"Yes, I was, Senator."

"Then, your position as a young child in New Orleans was not much different from the millions of child immigrants we now have in this country today, was it?"

"I'm not sure what you're asking me, Senator, by different. It was certainly a different time. But I grew up an American, with all the rights and privileges any other youngster had. I might not have been here illegally, but . . ."

"Fair enough, Ms. Chatrier," he said, showing some lack of respect by cutting her off. "But what I want to know is do you think it's good that everyone born in this country should automatically become a citizen?"

All right, she said to herself, the game is on. "I think that's a question for the people and their representatives in Congress to decide, whether to amend the Constitution in that regard."

"I'm asking you what you think."

Oh no you don't. "Senator, I'm flattered that you want my personal opinion, but why is my view of anymore interest than any other American?"

The senator paused, shook off some obvious annoyance, and then said, "Perhaps because you became a citizen through this very same provision."

"Well, I'm certainly blessed in that regard, Senator. You're absolutely right about that."

A few nodding heads and a snicker here and there came from those in the gallery who saw the back and forth as one up for Chatrier. The senator cleared his throat and peered at the nominee over his glasses, as if to say, *I thought we were on the same side.*

"All right then, can you tell me whether a law passed by Congress withholding citizenship from the children of illegal aliens, as has been suggested by some of my colleagues, should be upheld by the Supreme Court?"

That was the first Joan had heard of such a proposal. She figured he was making political mischief. In any case, the answer was not difficult. "The Fourteenth Amendment to the Constitution states very clearly that any person born in the United States is a citizen. It says nothing about who your parents are."

"So such a law should not be enforced by the court?"

"In my opinion, it would not be upheld."

"Then tell me if a law passed by Congress, which takes away all rights under our constitution from all aliens, legal and illegal, should be upheld by the court?"

"That's what happened in the 1880s, Senator, but it was slaves then, not illegal aliens. The Fourteenth Amendment was enacted to restore the constitutional rights of all persons."

"You're referring to the Dred Scott decision?"

"Yes."

"So, tell me then, Counselor, if all aliens, both illegal and permitted to be here, have all the rights of citizens, what's the point of having citizenship?"

Joan squashed a smile. "They don't have all the rights, Senator. In fact, illegal aliens, including those whose permits have expired, can be and are sent home under our current laws. But unlike most other long-standing democracies, France, for example, our Constitution refers to persons, not citizens, when it sets forth the protective clauses guarding the most basic rights. Those who are not citizens are still persons."

The Senator appeared to expect Joan's answer, and he moved quickly on to his next question. "Are you familiar, Ms. Chatrier, with the current tax bill before Congress?"

"Only what I've read in the press, Senator."

"I see," the Senator said, pausing to look down at his papers. He turned to address the chair. "Mr. Chairman, I had intended to explore some of the constitutional issues that have been raised in the Senate concerning the proposed new tax law. Upon reflection, I'm not sure this is the time or place to do that. I'd like the record to reflect this statement."

The chair nodded assent to the request, and the senator turned back to Joan. "I do have a question for you along these general lines, however. Can you tell me, Ms. Chatrier, what is socially more important, a person's . . . and notice, please, that I didn't use the term citizen . . . ." More light laughter from the gallery and an appreciative smile from Joan. "What is more important, Ms. Chatrier, a person's freedom from prejudice or that same person's bank balance?"

Joan took her coached long breath. *Clever by a mile was that question. You are black but rich, he'd said. Where does that place you on my roster of jurists?* She wondered if those watching had caught the real thrust of his question, but then addressed his point. "Senator, that's the kind of question my Mama always told me never to try to answer. It's darned if I do, and darned if I don't. But I'll say this, I can't help it if someone doesn't like the color of my skin, but I can sure do something about my bank balance if I have a mind to."

"Please, ladies and gentlemen," the chair said amidst clapping and some cheering. "I'm going to call a recess, and I'd like the marshals to bring some order to the assembly."

Joan watched as the senator stood up and left as quickly as he'd come.

PUERTO RICO

The senator from one of the southeastern states, who next took his turn before the appointee, was the one who wanted to adjourn the hearing until more information could be obtained about the nominee's time in San Juan, Puerto Rico.

"You spent several years at school in Puerto Rico, Ms. Chatrier, is that correct?"

"Yes."

"This was before attending law school?"

"Yes."

"I understand you were a good student, near the top of your class, in fact."

Joan blushed, but answered, "Yes."

"Why did you go to the islands to get your education?"

"I was given a full scholarship, and it was not as expensive as living here. We didn't have much money, Senator."

"I see. What did you do off campus while you were there in school? What were your activities?"

She knew the senator's staff had done their homework, but she was ready. "I played some volleyball, was on the debating team, and I wrote for the school paper."

"Were you involved in politics?"

"Not directly, Senator, but I had a paying job with one of the on-campus groups that touted independence for Puerto Rico."

"Doing what, Ms. Chatrier?"

"Writing mostly, editing articles that espoused their cause."

"You said *their* cause, Ms. Chatrier. Was it your cause, too?"

"I could understand why some of them wanted independence, but it wasn't clear thinking. If you look at the rest of the Caribbean, you can readily see what the economics would be like."

"What was your interest in that movement, Ms. Chatrier?"

"You mean personally?"

"Yes, personally."

"I had no personal interest. A couple of the young women who were involved in the group were friends of mine, and I needed a paying job to help cover expenses."

"Were you aware that this group advocated overthrowing the government of Puerto Rico?"

"Of course. How else would they get independence?" she said amongst titters from the gallery. "Puerto Rico became a U.S. territory at the same time as the Philippines and Cuba and are both independent now."

The senator looked at Joan, as if saying, *I don't need a history lesson from you, Ms. Chatrier.* He became testy. "Okay then, perhaps you were aware that a young man who worked for the FBI was killed by that group of friends of yours."

It serves you right for being contentious with him. Cool it, she admonished herself. "Senator, I was aware allegations were made that a man found dead on the beach at some hotel was an FBI informant, and that he reportedly had infiltrated one of the three main political parties, I guess the one advocating independence, and that he allegedly was killed to keep him from passing on information to Washington about protests that were planned. I never put much stock in the story."

"Did you know this man?"

"No."

"Did you not go to Havana, Cuba with him?"

"I've never been to Havana, Cuba, Senator."

"Never?"

"No, Senator, never."

The staff member seated in the back row behind the senator handed him a paper.

"I have here a statement from a Ms. Virginia Holton. Does that name ring a bell?"

"I'm afraid not, Senator."

"Well, Ms. Holton says here, in an affidavit sworn before my staff, that she was a friend of yours in San Juan, and that you and she and the FBI informant who was murdered, all three of you, went to Havana during Christmas break in your last year at the university. Do you deny that?"

"I've never been to Havana, Senator."

"Then this woman is lying?"

"If she says I went with her to Havana, she is mistaken."

"Were you aware during your time associated with the independence movement in Puerto Rico that much of the support for that movement was coming out of Cuba?"

"No, Senator, I was not."

At this point, Joan's mother, Mari Roland, watching at home, turned up the volume on her television set and went into the kitchen to make herself a stiff drink. She knew Joan had never been to Cuba, because Mari had talked her out of going. "Stay out of Cuba, Joan. You're an American citizen. You're not allowed to be there." The subject had not come up again.

When Mari returned to her seat and restored sound to her set, the senator was shuffling more papers. Finally, he brought one to the top of the pile in front of him, and then promptly ignored it.

"Ms. Chatrier, do I have the constitutional right to tell a lie?"

This question caused a soft ripple among the gallery, because some thought this was an indirect way of accusing Joan of having just lied to the committee about not visiting Havana.

Joan ignored the implication, and answered the question. "You have the right to speak your mind. If it turns out that what you say is untrue, there may be consequences if others are hurt or you're under oath. And a properly drawn law making those consequences, intended or unintended, would not be unconstitutional as a deprivation of your right to make the statement in the first place."

"So I don't have the right, the unqualified right, to tell a lie?"

The murmurs grew to an outright "boo," and the chairman, not without some sympathy for those complaining, raised his hand for quiet.

Joan smiled and responded. "You have the right to cause yourself grief, but not necessarily to do the same to others."

"So who decides what I say is not true?"

"You do, in the first instance, and eventually a court or jury when and if the matter comes properly before it."

"The press seems to be climbing on Joan's bandwagon," Charles Black told the President.

"What does Minturn think?"

"He's still out there on that limb."

"What else do you hear?"

"Well, the blogosphere is solidly on her side, too. Except for those writers who seem to be forever negative on all subjects, she's getting a positive following, according to my web surfing spies."

"What else?"

"It's mostly wait-and-see in the Senate. I think she's too good to be true for some, and they're waiting for the inevitable bad penny to show up."

"What about this trip to Havana business that came out this morning? Is that just another Senatorial witch hunt?"

"I don't know. I'll follow up with Gordon."

"Have you spoken with Gordon recently?"

"Not recently, but that reminds me . . . I hear rumbling from some sources about his wife-to-be . . . that her days as a law clerk are numbered."

"Of course, she was clerk to Justice Goode."

"That's part of it. But the problem is, she is being singled out by the senior senator from Illinois as being involved in the murder of a journalist in Chicago."

"Have you talked to Gordon about it?"

"Yes. They say it's all due to the man's mother, who has reasons for not liking Kate much."

"Just tell me if it's a real problem or not."

"Not yet."

The President looked at her chief of staff with an expression that told him that was no answer, and he ought to know better.

"Gordon will tell me if it becomes relevant."

She nodded an okay, and moved on to the next subject.

SWORN IN

Kate and Gordon piled into one of the long line of taxis waiting to pick up attendees leaving Justice Chatrier's swearing-in ceremony.

"She got off to a good start, didn't she?" Kate said as Gordon waved through the car window to a passing friend. "Did you notice the way several people there, the chief justice senior clerk, for example, were giving us the fisheye?"

"People are always looking at you, my love . . . and I don't blame them."

"Some were eyeing you, too, in case you didn't notice."

"You're not getting paranoid on me, are you?"

"Ha, ha. Maybe, but it's been happening in chambers a lot. They seem to think my film on the Cuban embargo three years ago started something. In their minds, it connects me to Joan Chatrier."

"You mean her article?"

"Yes, we're on the same page in their book."

Gordon had not mentioned Charles Black's information about the rumors circulating among the hardliner anti-Castro caucus and the President's opposition . . . that Kate and he, along with the White House, had cooked up a plot to get rid of Justice Goode so they could put Chatrier on the court before the case on the validity of the Cuban embargo came up on appeal.

It would do no good to bring that nonsense up. "Well, I guess they can think what they want, Kate. It's their problem . . . for now, anyway," and he changed the subject. "How are you fixed for a few days in Bermuda? I think we both deserve a little R & R."

"I could go over the weekend, maybe."

"Memorial Day is Monday. See if they can do without their junior clerk at large for three days, and we'll come back on Tuesday. It's only an hour and half flight."

"Sounds wonderful. I'll ask his assistant this afternoon. Who knows? The way things are going, maybe they'll ask me not to come back."

That night, instead of going home to Gordon's gourmet cooking, they went out on the town.

"Gordon, that was fun. I didn't know you were such a good friend of the publisher, Bernard."

"One of the nicer men in town, Kate. He and I go back to the summer I worked on the President's primary run for the Senate."

"The one she lost?"

"She didn't get the party's nomination in a bad year for them, but he and I lived on the same college campus the rest of that year and the next. We picked it up again four years ago when she decided to make a run for the presidency."

"He seemed to have figured it all out in Joan's case."

"He doesn't miss much, Kate, but what he thinks privately and what he prints are not bound together. He accents the positive. That's what makes his magazine so readable. He likes you, by the way."

"Because I was with you, Turkey," Kate said, shaking her head but smiling.

"I don't think so. He does his homework."

"So what did he say when his wife and I went to the ladies' room?" She'd thought the man had something on his mind when his wife said, "Want to join me in the ladies', Kate?"

"He asked me if Joan Chatrier would let an acquaintance of his write an article on her life for his magazine, beginning at the beginning and through her confirmation to the court."

Kate thought this strange, but there was a lot she didn't know about what went around in Washington. "Who?" she asked.

"His name is Byron Colder."

"Never heard of him. Why'd Bernard ask you?"

"People seem to be put off dealing directly with Supreme Court justices."

"What did you tell him?"

"I said, why not? I told him I'd speak with Charles Black about it first, and then Joan."

Kate nodded and yawned. "What time are your meetings tomorrow?"

"Eight-thirty."

"We better tuck you in, big boy."

Following three days in Bermuda and sporting her first tan in over a year, Kate didn't mind being asked to help prepare the office for the incoming Justice Chatrier. It wasn't a male/female thing, but she overheard one of the law clerks say it was logical since they both thought the Cuban embargo had been unconstitutional. Two of Justice Goode's other law clerks had moved on to law firm jobs in New York and Chicago. The long weekend in Bermuda with Gordon had recharged her batteries, and she dove into helping Joan get her office organized.

Boxes began to arrive, filing cabinets were set up, and Joan's desk was delivered as the retiring justice moved out to his family home in the horse country of Virginia. A private line was put in place for Justice Chatrier in a newly constructed small alcove off her main office. Kate arranged the items as the court's newest justice had instructed, including her private laptop and collections of addresses and telephone numbers. The additional privacy afforded seemed unnecessary, but Kate thought it was none of her business and kept such notions to herself.

"Kate, hello, it's so nice to have your help," Joan Chatrier said, coming into the office and dropping an armful of files on a table in the corner. "You're doing such a good job on this office. I very much appreciate it."

"No problem, Your Honor. I'm happy to help."

"Thank you, Kate. I'm coming in over the weekend, and I'll do the fine-tuning then," Chatrier said, but then remembering something, continued. "There is one thing. My mother will call later today, around five. I can't be here, but she'll leave a message. Could you check to see if that message comes through the new telephone setup? If it doesn't, give me a call over at the law school so I'll know. Mother will be upset if she doesn't think her message was recorded. She and I are all the other has these days."

"I understand, Your Honor. I'll take care of it."

"Let's dispense with the 'Your Honor' formality, Kate, when we're not where the rest of the world sees us."

She smiled and nodded, still not comfortable addressing the new justice by her first name. "I'll make sure your phone message hook-up is working."

Joan Chatrier's mother called right on schedule, but Kate was busy at that moment in conference with the justice who'd taken over one of the opinions Kate had been working on with Justice Goode. When they were finished, she returned to the alcove where Joan's private line had been installed and played back the message. The lady's voice came through clearly with a noticeable French accent that surprised Kate, but the woman had signed off as required. No problem, and no need to call the justice at her office across town.

Good thing, too, she thought, *I don't have her number over there*. She leafed through Chatrier's private notebook for the number. She found it after a few moments, but as she closed the book she noticed something that confused and then startled her.

She dismissed several times that afternoon, and during her walk home, doing something with what she'd noticed. She started to ask Gordon during dinner, but she wasn't sure discussing the subject with him wouldn't be a violation of her duty to the court, and get them both in hot water. *That was a first . . . putting the court before her man.*

"What's bothering you, Kate? You seem distracted . . . that three days at Mid Ocean with a tennis racket in your hand again do you in? By the way, the kids at the club thought you should turn pro."

She laughed at Gordon's remark, and then dealt in a little subterfuge. "I was just thinking . . . and those three days were glorious, Darling. I loved every minute of it . . . it's just with Joan Chatrier at the court now . . . I don't really feel comfortable. It's strange, and I don't understand why I feel this way."

Gordon placed knife and fork on his plate and leaned back. "What happened, Kate? Was Joan in chambers today? Did you speak with her?"

"She came in for a while. I'm helping her get things organized."

"Joan can be pretty demanding. She had a reputation around the office."

"No, no, she was fine."

"So what's changed by her being on the court?"

Kate wasn't hungry. She put her napkin on the table and looked at Gordon. "Can we talk about this tomorrow?"

"Sure, but we usually get the issues out while they're hot."

"I know, but I need to think about this one. It's no big deal, Gordon. I do want to talk about it with you . . . but not tonight. Okay, my love?"

"Sure. I'm here when you need me." He got up from the table and gave Kate a bear hug before they cleared the table together.

Later that evening, before retiring to the bedroom, Kate made the decision to call Detective Julia Gold in the morning on her cell phone.

BACK ON THE SOUTHSIDE

"Ms. Stevens! What can I do for you?" Julia Gold said. "How are things in our nation's capitol?"

"Things are okay here, Detective. I saw on the news last night that you're having some stormy weather in Chicago. It made me think of you."

"They don't call this the Windy City for nothing, Counselor. I'm always flattered when people think of me. I hope you're calling to tell me what your friend Judd Arnold was doing in Chicago."

"Detective Gold, I have to tell you that Mrs. Arnold has hatched a real vendetta against me. You must have heard all the noise one of your senators is making because of her accusations."

"I'm afraid I can't do much about that, Ms. Stevens . . . say, may I call you Katherine?"

"Kate. Please call me Kate."

"Well Kate, I know what that woman has been trying to do. We don't pay much attention, but I guess in Washington this sort of stuff is what the politicians live on. I'm sorry. Maybe if we can advance the ball a bit more toward finding out what he was doing here . . . "

Kate saw her opening. "I'm probably going to be out of a job soon. My justice retired, and the court doesn't much like its law clerks getting involved in murders and things. I wonder if I could appoint myself as Judd Arnold's lawyer, and take up the cause. Maybe I could be of help."

There was no immediate response from Gold's end of the line, so Kate continued with her argument.

"Of course I only mean figuratively."

"Keep talking," Kate heard the detective say.

"Yes, well, I knew Judd. I know how he thinks . . . I mean thought. You said he was over here on a story. Do you know what it was about? Who did he speak to here in Washington before going to Chicago? Did he call home? If not, why not? And, very important, where are his notes? Did he use a computer in the *Times* D.C. office? Would that turn up any names or ideas he brought from New Orleans . . . isn't that where you said his story was centered? Wasn't he in New Orleans before coming here to Washington?" These were all questions and thoughts that Kate knew Julia Gold must have also considered. She waited.

"Sure. Of course. If you can find answers, I'll share them with you. I can't really show you our files, but frankly, there's not a hell of a lot in there."

Kate was warming up. She was in the church. Now she needed to find the right pew. "Can you share with me the names of the persons at the *Times* in D.C. and the *Trib* in Paris . . . the persons that you've spoken with? I'll be discrete."

Another pause, while Gold obviously weighed the pluses and minuses. "Yeah, okay, I'll send you the names of the D.C. staff that I was told were with Judd Arnold over that weekend, but I want a report back after you've spoken with them. I had a phone conversation with one of them and got no joy from the session. Maybe you can charm something out of them."

"That's a deal, Detective."

"Call me Julia, Kate."

"Okay, Julia. One more thing."

"Shoot."

"Where is 108th Street in Chicago?"

In her Chicago office, Julia Gold sat open-mouthed, a puzzled look on her face. She tugged at an earlobe with one hand as she replaced the handset with the other. The place where Arnold's body had been found was marked on the map she kept in the top drawer of her desk. She checked the cross streets nearest to the site, and was about to call Kate Stevens back when that thought was interrupted by another.

Was this the connection she'd been waiting for? The conspiracy that brought Judd Arnold to Chicago, and Kate Stevens, under all this pressure, had decided to own up? Or had this bright woman seen something they'd all missed? If Kate didn't call in the next day or so, Julia was sure as hell going to call her.

That evening, Kate made good on her promise to Gordon. She approached the moment with some apprehension. Didn't he know where Joan's mother lived? And if so, how come he hadn't put Judd's Chicago together with Joan's?

"Better make yourself a martini, Darling. I'll have one, too."

"You're pregnant!"

She laughed. "No, but I am quite afraid of what else I might have stumbled into."

"What is it?"

"First, the martini."

Gordon got up and made the second martini he'd ever given to Kate. He made one for himself, too. Then he sat across from her at the kitchen table. He wore a suppressed smile that was given away by the fire in his eyes.

She took a very small sip and crinkled her nose. "How do you drink these things?"

"The second sip's always better," he said, taking a bit of his own. "So, what's up?"

The tension built in Kate's demeanor. "Where does Joan Chatrier's mother live? Do you know?"

Gordon looked at her. "I should know, shouldn't I?" he said absently, tilting his head and moving his jaw back and forth the way Kate knew he did when working out a puzzle. "I'm thinking Evanston, Illinois or Chicago. Why?" He paused, cocking his head to one side again and looking more intensely at her. "Chicago. That's an interesting place," he said.

Kate took a deep breath and nodded. "Yes, it is. Yesterday, Joan Chatrier asked me to check her telephone answering service on the private line she had installed in her office at court. She said her mother was going to call her around five, and if the recording didn't work, I was to call Joan right away."

"At GW."

"Yes. Well, the call came through okay, and I thought that was good, because she forgot to give me her number at the school. So I checked the phonebook next to the answering machine, and copied that number from her contact list so I'd have it next time."

"I'm sure she wouldn't mind your doing that, Kate."

"No, that's not it."

Gordon took another swallow of his drink.

She squinted, sipped her martini, set her glass on the table, and took another deep breath. "As I closed Joan's phonebook, I couldn't help notice the back side of an envelope that was stuck in there with her mother's name and return address on it."

Gordon's expression said, "And?"

"That address, Gordon, is on the Southside of Chicago."

His eyes reflected something close to keen interest, and he seemed to know where she was heading.

"Gordon, if it really is her mother's address, it's not far from the alley where Judd Arnold's body was found."

Gordon's smile was gone. "It must be a pretty long street, but that would be one hell of a coincidence."

"I know coincidence is not high on your list of credible happenings." She picked up her glass and took an honest sip of her drink. "Think back. Did we ever mention anything to Joan about Judd?"

Gordon's cheeks went concave like he sucked on a lemon. "Not as far as I recall."

Kate had made up her mind. "As you say, that's probably a very long street. I'm going out on a limb here, but I think Judd went to Chicago to interview or confront Joan Chatrier's mother."

Gordon was of the school that ideas and information need to be carefully examined before being exposed to light. Gordon took another sip of his martini. "I see what you've been wrestling with."

She rose from her chair and walked in a circle, thinking out loud. "There's something there, Gordon. It's not just a big coincidence, and I can't let it go. Judd had just come from New Orleans. Joan was born to Mari in that city. There's a connection. I just know it."

"Are you saying that Joan or her mother killed Judd Arnold?" Gordon watched Kate pace back and forth.

"Goodness, no. What I'm saying is that there's a connection between what took Judd to Chicago and what he was doing in New Orleans, and I think it's too much of a coincidence that the newest member of the Supreme Court came from that same city and has a mother who lives near where Judd's body was found."

Gordon sat back on his haunches and took a swallow of his drink. "What kind of a story was Judd Arnold working on?"

"I don't know, but I'm going over to the *Times* tomorrow and talk to the two or three staffers with whom Judd apparently spent time here in D.C. that weekend we were in New York . . . ." Suddenly she remembered the phone call she'd been too late to pick up. "That was Judd calling as we came in the door from Reagan. Remember the call I couldn't trace?"

He nodded. Not a happy nod from the tense expression on his face.

"I'm going over there tomorrow."

"Kate, I'm not sure that's wise."

"Why?"

"You shouldn't get involved. Let the Chicago police handle it."

"They're hamstrung by the Chicago politicians and Ad Arnold. They're not going to take anything they get from me. Ad Arnold's seen to that. No . . . I've got to do this myself . . . until I have something concrete."

"The chief justice is not going to like it if word gets around you're playing cop. You know what a small town political Washington is."

"I sure do, my Darling. Because of those damn politics I was asked to pack up my desk this afternoon. They suggested maybe I'd like to join Justice Goode in retirement. Now, I've got nothing to do but help find the sonofabitch who killed Judd Arnold."

The thought that Kate would have something that she was passionate about to keep her busy until they both agreed the time had come to go on with her career in the law was a good thing. "Okay, Kate, get it out of your system. Who knows, maybe you'll solve the murder in the process. You have my complete support."

She said thanks and went into the den to plot her visit to the *Times* D.C. news office.

She dressed simply, but elegantly, and knocked on the door of the man Julia Gold told her had spent time with Judd Arnold during the days he'd spent in D.C. before taking off for Chicago. The name on the door, however, did not match the man in the room.

"Jack's not here," the guy said, but taking a good look at the vision before him, added, "Maybe I can help you. The name's Ben," and he held out his hand.

"Hi, Ben," Kate said with her best smile, and paused to put the right words together. "An old and very good friend of mine was here several weeks ago on a story for the *Times Herald Tribune* in Paris. Maybe you met him. His name was Judd Arnold." She crossed her fingers and waited.

"Judd Arnold? No. I can't say I remember that name, but . . . yeah, was he the bloke who got himself killed out in Chicago? I guess we've all heard about that."

"Yes," Kate said, wiping off the smile and replacing it with the right amount of sadness. "That was Judd. We were at Georgetown together."

Ben looked more carefully at Kate, and perked up. "And I bet you're the girlfriend that this guy's mother is always complaining about."

Now Kate laughed. She couldn't help it . . . the way he said it made Ad Arnold seem so irrelevant.

"I guess you know the whole story, Ben. Maybe you *can* help me."

Ben smiled and nodded. "Sure, but you know the Chicago police are all over this business, and they've been to see our editors in New York."

"I know. Detective Julia Gold of the Chicago homicide division gave me Jack's name. I'm here to see if I can help move their investigation along. You can call her if you want."

Ben seemed to be enjoying the intrigue that Kate was injecting into his daily routine. "Exactly what are you looking for?"

"I'm afraid it's more like a fishing exhibition. Judd came here from New Orleans, according to Detective Gold, but no one seems to know what he was doing in Chicago."

Ben followed without comment.

"I knew Judd pretty well. The detective and I think that if I knew more about what he was researching in New Orleans, we might be able to piece together a scenario for Chicago. Did you see him when he was here?"

"Not to speak with, but I can tell you who I think did . . . Mary Watts. She's here . . . right down the hall."

Kate added up the score back in the den on her side of the community desk she and Gordon shared. She spread out her papers and notes and put together what she had.

Four . . . almost five . . . weeks in New Orleans. That was a long time. The story he was assigned from Paris was to capture, using local characters and a legend or two, here and there, to give credence to the belief that New Orleans maintained to this day a common vein with France. He had originally intended to be in New Orleans three weeks, but called Paris to ask for another 10 days, which evolved into two weeks before he was killed. He was secretive during the time in the D.C. office, so much so that it became a joke. They all, especially Mary Watts, wanted to know what it was like working in Paris for the Trib, *but all Judd wanted to do was scour the* Times *editions for each day in the fol-*

lowing three weeks. He made copies of various articles and threw them into his briefcase. Then he had sent from Paris some articles from the Tribune. *Mary thought it looked like he was trying to tie in some other French colonies or pageantry to round out his story. He had his air ticket changed while he was here . . . from Washington to New York to Paris to direct back to Paris. So he must have bought another ticket to fly to Chicago. Mary thought he had a credit card, but she wasn't sure. The* Tribune *didn't provide cards, so if he had one it must have been his own. Mary also recalled that Judd had a cell phone that was not company issue. That was about it.*

Kate made a very brief synopsis from her notes. Then she had a brainstorm. What was in the news between the time Judd landed in New Orleans and arrived in D.C.? What happened that might have caused him to extend his visit, and what was he looking for as he scoured the *Times* editions back in D.C.? Were the two the same? She logged on her Nexus account and searched this time period, which was now almost three months prior.

Bingo. My Dad always said it was better to be lucky than smart. What was the connection? All the talk in New York Times *and* Washington Post *circles about the likely candidates to replace Justice Goode, if he decided to retire. Every day, day after day, moving even the terrorist activities and wars from the lead column on the first page.*

Judd, in the middle of his story on the Frenchness of New Orleans had seen that one of its children, Joan Chatrier, married to a Frenchman retired from the Foreign Service, and herself born in New Orleans, was a candidate, granted a very remote one at that point, for the High Court. He must have burst with the possibilities this offered for a journalist, who burned to be on the news desk of a major paper.

But now Kate had a problem. What would Gordon think? The spotlight would shift from Judd's mother and herself to Joan Chatrier and her mother in Chicago. This would not be without political consequences when the press started rabble-rousing about why Judd had been killed. Nor was this something that Gordon and his friends in the White House needed following the successful confirmation of Joan to the court.

COUNT ME OUT

Julia Gold had Chief Donovan's attention.

"So the Stevens woman thinks this reporter might have spiced up a piece he was writing on New Orleans by tying in the new Supreme Court justice."

Julia wanted to keep the case of Judd Arnold's killing on the division's priority list. "It would explain his presence in Chicago."

"True enough, Gold, but it doesn't get us beyond his being mugged in an alley. Even if he did come here to see the Judge's mother—and we don't have any reason why he wanted to do that—there's no evidence that he did. It's been months now, and nothing has come out about him or his story. Hell, the FBI has been all over these people with their investigation."

"That's why we need to talk with Mrs. Roland, Chief."

"Why should we listen to the Stevens woman? She's just trying to get out from under all these accusations."

"I don't think that's it, Chief. What's the harm in my seeing what the justice's mother has to add to our empty bucket of information?"

Donovan slapped the table with his open hand. "No, and I don't have time to talk about this. I'm taking that house and the Roland woman off limits, Gold. I'm not having a hundred reporters around here, asking why one of my detectives is questioning the black immigrant mother of a Supreme Court justice. This is Chicago, Gold."

With nothing further to go on, the chief left the Arnold case on the back burner.

Julia called Kate as she'd promised, hoping at the same time to stir up something more to add to the circumstances of her case. "The *Tribune* in Paris repeated what they told me before," Julia said. "Arnold was doing a human interest series on the French background of New Orleans. He had no business here in Chicago, and as far as they knew, he had no plans to come here. We don't have enough to bring in Mari Roland for questioning."

"But it's still an amazing coincidence," Kate said, "that Joan Chatrier was born in New Orleans and her husband was French."

"But what did Arnold have to say to the justice's mother, if that's why he came to Chicago?" Julia knew she needed a more direct connection.

"Maybe because Joan would be too young to remember much about New Orleans. Or maybe it would be going too far too fast for Judd to call Joan directly. The mother could fill in those early years spent in New Orleans."

Not enough, Julia thought, but she told Kate, "Yeah, I guess. Anyway, we're punting on the case. My priorities have been reassigned. We haven't closed the file, but my chief is still betting it was a street mugging."

Gordon told Kate when she reported her conversation with Gold, "Hey, if the Chicago police don't think your *what-if* scenario is sufficiently noteworthy to put the case back on the front burner, I'm certainly not going to bother Charles Black and the President with it."

Kate nodded. "I don't blame you," she said, but the empty feeling in her stomach wouldn't go away. She was more sure than ever that a connection existed between Judd Arnold's death and Joan Chatrier. She knew, however, that it was much too explosive an issue to start belaboring Gordon, let alone to go public with her convictions.

Julia Gold did a u-turn in the police car, returning to look at the house owned by Mari Roland. She parked down the street, removing from her briefcase the list she'd made weeks earlier during her interviews of people in the neighborhood. No one at this house had answered her ring back in April. She decided this was as good a time as any to close the circle on that aspect of the investigation. Closing the file was her excuse for disobeying the chief's orders. He couldn't object too much to her following department procedures, even if it was a ruse to gain access to the house.

The tall, gray-haired woman who came to the door towered over Julia as she held out her badge.

"What do you want?" the woman asked in a pleasant, but no non-sense, tone.

She didn't let on she knew the woman's name. "I'm Detective Gold, Ma'am. I'm with the Chicago police department. We're investigating a sus-picious death in this neighborhood. I knocked on your door a couple of months ago, but I guess you weren't in. We still haven't discovered the iden-tity of the victim," she said, beginning with a bit of mischief to mask her intentions, "or what he was doing here on this street," she finished, putting the emphasis on "this."

The woman was resolute. "I can't help you."

"Did any of your neighbors mention that I was here before?"

"We don't talk much," the woman said.

"Not even to the mother of a Supreme Court justice?" she asked on impulse.

The woman froze. Julia watched her left hand slip off the inside door-knob and dangle at her side.

"Who told you that?" the woman asked, scowling at Julia.

She'd gone too far. This was the substance of a reprimand. It was her impatience with the whole damn business, but the fear she now felt pro-duced the energy to keep going.

"It was on the news. Certainly you saw it." In fact, she wasn't sure that any local newscast had pointed to Justice Chatrier's mother as a resident of Chicago, let alone in this section of the Southside.

"It was not. My daughter promised . . ." The woman stopped, realizing she'd let the cat out of the bag.

"You should be proud of your daughter. I certainly am," she said. "We should have more women like her."

Mari Roland stood erect and stiff-backed in the doorway.

Gold wanted to get inside. "Ms. Roland, may I have your autograph?"

"Don't be stupid."

"Really, I think it's wonderful we have the mother of a Supreme Court justice living right here in our town."

"I'm not going to give you an autograph. That's dumb."

"All right, Ms. Roland. I can respect your desire for privacy, but I need to know where you were on Tuesday, the sixth of April."

Julia had crossed way beyond the line of her authority. There'd be no excuse that the chief would accept now. There was also nothing more to be lost by continuing.

"What?" Mari Roland said. "Why do you want to know that? Do you remember where you were on that day?"

She did remember. "As I said, Ms. Roland, a man was found dead right around the corner from where we're standing, and we want to know what he was doing here."

"I told you. I don't know anything about it."

It's odd the way she said that . . . just like all the guilty people Julia had ever interviewed. She dismissed the thought as her grasping for something that wasn't there. And there was nothing to be gained by badgering.

"What's your phone number, Ms. Roland?"

"It's unlisted."

"But you do have a phone?"

"What business is it of yours?"

"I may need to call you."

"Don't."

She tried a bluff. "Ms. Roland, I can retrieve your number from the phone company. Why don't you save me the trouble?"

"Then will you leave?"

"Yes, if you give me your correct number. If you don't, I'll be back with a warrant." The same warrant she knew her chief would never authorize.

"Wait here, I'll get a paper and write it down for you."

She disobeyed her instructions, following the woman into a small all-purpose room, which, with a kitchen, a closet, and a half bath, was all there was to the first floor of the modest, two-story, brick cottage. The room looked even smaller because of a full-sized grand piano in the corner. On the piano was the photograph of a young woman in cap and gown, holding a diploma of some sort in her hand. Behind the young woman in the picture was a college tower that could have been the law school at The University of Pennsylvania.

"I didn't invite you into my home, Detective," Mari Roland said, coming back into the room and handing Julia a card with a number on it. The woman stood firmly in place as Julia took the card.

"Please send my congratulations to your daughter, Ms. Roland," she said. "You don't mind if I come back when we have more information?"

"You now have my telephone number. You have some time before I change it again."

Cute, Julia thought. "I'll try to give you some notice."

She took another good look around the first floor as she retraced her steps and left Mari Roland's home, trying without success to make a connection between the woman whose photo was on the grand piano with the larger than life character that presumed to be her mother. What was the mother of a Supreme Court justice doing in that house? One part of Julia didn't want to find anything bad there, but something wasn't right . . . and that awareness nagged at her for days.

Several young children were gathered around the police car when Julia reached it. "Hi, kids, how're you doing?"

"Can we blow the siren?" one of the children asked.

"That's not a very good idea," she said, smiling. "Do you know the story of the boy who cried 'wolf'?"

"I do," answered a young girl.

Julia nodded, encouraging her to explain.

"A boy was always saying the wolf was coming. He did it to scare his friends," the girl said, "so when the wolf really did come, nobody believed him."

"That's very good, young lady. What's your name?"

"Glory. I'm in third grade."

"Well, you're a very smart young lady." She turned to a boy in the group. "Don't you think so?"

"I'm smarter than she is," the boy said.

"Oh, no, you're not," said the girl.

"Yes, I am." He pointed to the Roland house. "You came to see the lady in that house. I know why, too."

"Oh," Julia said. "How do you know that?"

"You're looking for that man's package. That's why."

"What do you mean his package?"

"I saw him take it," he said, pointing.

"JJ," the little girl said, "Mama said not to talk about that. I'm going to tell." She ran off to tell her mother.

Julia squatted down and looked into the boy's eyes. "What did you see, young man?"

"I was playing my game when he went into that house."

"Who? Who did you see?"

"He was dressed funny."

"You mean he had a suit and a necktie?" Julia put her hands up to her throat like she'd watched her father tighten his necktie.

The boy nodded. "Yes."

"Was he an old man?"

He shook his head, and raised his hand up in the air.

"He was tall?"

The boy nodded.

"Did you see him come out?"

The boy shook his head again.

"What game were you playing?" she asked to keep the boy interested.

"Betting on cars' licenses."

"That sounds like a fun game. Did you win?" She smiled.

"I always win," the boy said with a nod, returning her smile.

"Did the man arrive in a car?"

The boy nodded.

"What kind of car was it?"

"It was a taxi, but those don't count in my game."

"I see. Well, did that taxi wait until the man came out?"

"No."

"And you didn't see the man come out?"

The boy had just enough time to repeat, "No," when his mother arrived and scooped him up.

"Let him alone, Officer," the mother said as she carted him off.

WRIGLEY FIELD

"I know we can't use the kid as a witness, Chief, but sure as hell we've found out the Arnold guy was in that house. We've got enough to get a warrant and search the place."

"Gold, what that little boy says he saw happened more than six weeks ago. That makes him unreliable. How many other people on other days went into that house? Forget it."

Not very many, Julia thought. "We need to get in there," she pressed.

"And what do you expect to find . . . besides ten dozen reporters asking why the Chicago PD is searching the home of the mother of the newest Supreme Court justice? I told you to stay away from her."

"We have an obligation, Chief. You should hear yourself talk."

"Okay, that does it. Detective Gold, I've managed to survive around here by not causing anymore grief than necessary, and this would bring you and me more grief than . . . hell . . . even more than having that damn woman from Hempstead, Long Island on the phone ten times a day. Let it go. That lady and her daughter did not kill Judd Arnold. You know it, and I know it."

Julia hadn't reached the end of Chief Donovan's rope . . . not yet. "But we don't know it," she said with emphasis on "know." "Maybe it wasn't murder. It might have been an accident."

He gazed at her over the rim of his glasses. "Did that blow on the back of Arnold's head look like an accident?"

She'd pushed as far as she dared. "Okay, Chief, but is it all right if I call the woman in Washington who tipped us on this?"

"Don't let the press get wind of it, though, or you're looking at a long, unscheduled vacation."

Kate paced the apartment. Why had Gordon picked this night to be so late? She needed to speak with him, and the subject did not suit the phone . . . especially a cell phone.

Gordon found her sound asleep in a chair in front of the TV with an ad selling erectile dysfunction drugs blazing away.

"Oh, you're home," she said when he gently woke her with a kiss on the forehead, and turned off the television with the remote that lay in her lap.

"I had to finish the motion papers on the Myers case," he said. "We go before Judge Wilson in the morning. Why aren't you in bed?"

"I had to speak with you. I received another call from Detective Gold in Chicago."

"Can I get something to eat first?"

"I brought home a pizza. I can heat it up for you."

"Okay, come into the kitchen, where we beard the lions."

She laughed and followed Gordon, who turned on the lights as he went.

"So this detective thinks Joan's mother had something to do with Judd Arnold's death."

"She isn't there yet. Anyway, her chief has put the clamps on."

"Why?" Gordon said, taking two pieces of pizza out of the oven. "Either she's involved or not. What are they afraid of?"

"The only evidence she has is a small boy's testimony that he saw a white man in a suit and tie going into her house. He doesn't remember exactly when, and he's not too clear on the other details; only that the man was dressed like Judd was when the police found his body. Detective Gold tried to get a look into Joan's mother's house, but all she saw was a grand piano with a graduation picture of Joan atop it."

"What does the detective want you to do?"

"How did you know that?" she said, wondering how she'd given away what she had on her mind.

"Oh, I don't know. Just a hunch."

"She wants me to ask Joan to ask her mother what Judd Arnold was doing in her home on the sixth of April."

"Oh, boy. What did you tell her?"

"I told her you'd need to handle that one. I said I'd think about asking you."

Gordon nodded, grappling with a wedge of pizza.

"What if I do ask her, she calls her mother, and is told no man like that was ever in her home. Then, what? Do we call Chicago and tell Gold that? You said it yourself earlier on. That gets us too involved. Why doesn't this detective call Joan herself?"

"I guess they won't let her."

"Then she ought to just drop it."

"Gordon, my Darling, Judd Arnold was a friend of mine. I'd like the person who killed him to be caught, tried, and convicted. And I'll tell you, this detective . . . Julia Gold is her name . . . is one sharp police officer. She thinks, without a doubt, that the Roland connection on 108th Street is linked to Judd's death. That's why they want to know whether Joan knew her mother received a visit from Judd."

"Then let them ask. That's her job."

"Sure, but she's asked for my help."

Gordon nodded, and then he changed the subject. "How are you getting on with Joan at court these days?"

It was a put off, but she trusted Gordon. She took a deep breath and answered. "Not getting on or off. She is ignoring my presence. It's quite unnerving."

"Have you tried making small talk with her?"

"I don't see her much. She has her own clerks now. Two came in this week."

"What does she say?"

"Nothing. The best I get is a quick nod. I don't know, maybe I'm paranoid. She's probably just too focused on what she's doing."

"Maybe she knows you blew the whistle in Chicago."

"What whistle did I blow? That her mother lives on the Southside of Chicago? Anyway, how could she know that?"

Gold combed through records of telephone calls made from Mari Roland's phone, arguing with herself as she compiled the record. *She calls her daughter in Washington every day at five o'clock in the afternoon. It's like clockwork, every day for month after month . . . five o'clock, not 5:15 or 4:45. But on that afternoon in April, she doesn't call at all. Her daughter calls her, but not until later that night. And you're telling me nothing went on in that house that Thursday afternoon?*

"It's all circumstantial," Chief Donovan said later when Julia gave him her report. "Would you bet your life on it, or your career? Because that's what you'll be doing. If you go on with this and end up accusing a justice of the Supreme Court of harboring a criminal . . . or worse, of aiding and abetting a murder, it's not just your career . . . I'll be walking a beat again to save my pension."

"What can I bring you, Chief, that'll change your mind?"

"How about a confession? No, no, forget I said that. I don't want you near her or that house on 108th. I mean it, Gold. Stay away from her. The Cubs are playing the Giants this afternoon. Don't you have a box? Take the afternoon off. And that's an order."

Donovan knew Julia's real priorities. The box at Wrigley Field that her father had turned over to her before he'd died was on the third base line, a few strides inside the bag. Her father had always told her this was the best spot, because you could not only see home plate, but you had a commanding view of runners rounding second and trying to score on a single into right field or a double to left center. On the first base side, you had the sun in your eyes and were too far away from the best action. He added, "and you get to catch a lot of foul balls." Julia loved being there and communing with her dad.

The stadium was full that day for a game with the San Francisco Giants, and a friend had brought along a couple of his business associates at her invitation. As she told a girlfriend, "You get hit on because you wear your skirt short. I get hit on for the Wrigley Box."

In all the years occupying these seats, Julia, her dad and friends had caught, or been hit by, more than a few dozen foul line drives and pop-ups down the third base line, but on this day her seats were on the delivery end of a splintered wooden bat swung by the great Barry Bonds of steroid and home run fame, which came flying through the air left of third base. They all ducked and avoided injury, but she hung on to the splintered bat. A busted bat swung by Barry Bonds would make a good conversation piece on the wall of her apartment.

On the drive home she had the sudden thought to make what was left of Bond's bat a gift to the small boy who'd tried to help her on the Arnold case, and who'd run into a lot of trouble because of it. The small boy had done a civic good deed, and Julia decided he deserved a reward.

She knocked on the front door a little after dinnertime and greeted his mother. "I thought he might like a bat broken by Barry Bonds. You might even see it on television tonight. It whistled into our seats, and almost took off our heads."

The woman looked unimpressed, but the boy jumped up and down, screaming with delight. He knew who Barry Bonds was, and begged his mother to let him stay up long enough to see the game's highlights on television.

She patted the young boy on the head, asking his mother if, someday, they'd all like to accompany her to a game.

As she wrapped up her brief stay, the boy emerged from behind his mother and handed something to Julia. It was a toy baseball bat, about eighteen inches long, the kind given to children to play with using a small rubber ball. It was wooden, like the broken Barry Bonds bat, and just as hard.

"Where'd you get that, JJ?" his mother demanded, because she'd not seen it before.

The boy looked up at Julia. "I found it down there," he said, pointing at the alley.

"Get back in the house, JJ." Turning to Julia, she said, "Don't you pay him no mind, Officer."

"Did you see who put it there?" she asked the boy.

"A dog was playing with it," he said. "You can see all the tooth marks. It was all slimy until I washed it off."

"When did this happen?" Julia asked.

"It was after school," he said.

"You mean the next day, after you saw the man go into that house?"

He was still nodding his head as his mother dragged him into the house and shut the door.

Julia placed the toy bat in a plastic bag and waited until the next morning, when she handed it over to the crime lab for whatever they could come up with. If the boy hadn't washed everything off, maybe they could put two and two together. She didn't have the same feeling about the bat that she'd had with the business card in Judd Arnold's suit coat pocket. The bat had been washed and handled. It was unlikely any material evidence could have survived if even there in the first place.

"I swear, Gold," Chief Donovan said as he walked past her desk on his way up to the commissioner's office for a meeting on how to handle what she'd found. "I don't know whether to fire your ass or to put you in for a citation."

Back in the lab, the technicians had tested the bat. It showed traces of skin cells in and around the trademark depressions, and these it turned out matched Judd Arnold's DNA. The boy had given Julia the hard object that had struck the back of Judd Arnold's head, and it had done so on the trademark depression where the skin cells had become embedded.

A SOUTHERN GENTLEMAN

Kate walked from the Supreme Court to Gordon's office on 17ᵗʰ Street NW after cleaning out her desk in chambers. Emily greeted her in the reception area.

"Hi, Kate . . . long time no see." Emily could see Kate was not her usual perky self. "He's in the big conference room," she said. "Come on, you can take over his office. I'll tell him you're here."

Kate was seated at Gordon's desk with a bottle of water and a note pad, compliments of Emily, when he returned. He gave her a hug, and she hung on to him for a long moment.

"Are you okay?"

"I am now," she said.

"What's going on?"

She explained a call she'd received from Julia Gold a few hours earlier.

"So Judd Arnold really was working on Joan's story, but apparently doing it on his own? How did the police work it out?"

"It seems Judd did have a girlfriend in Paris, after all. The woman, an Australian who'd been home on family business, came into the Paris office late yesterday to hand over some of Judd's things she thought they might want. The last she'd heard from Judd was a text message sent from the

121

phone that's never been found. He asked when she was due to be back in Paris, and told her he'd found something that would require him to remain in New Orleans a few days longer. Then, he called her from D.C. that he was going to Chicago."

Gordon squinted, his lower jaw moving like he had something stuck in his teeth. "Anything else?"

"Yes, Julia Gold came up with the murder weapon. It was found by the same kid who saw someone like Judd go into the Roland house," Kate said with a fleeting smile she hoped might be contagious. "I can give you my scenario, but maybe you'd better stick with the facts . . . such as they are."

Gordon shook his head. "So someone killed him to keep whatever he found a secret?"

"Judd must have found something," she said.

"Something that the FBI didn't come up with?"

The skepticism in Gordon's voice annoyed her. "You've been telling me forever how the agents miss things in these background checks on presidential appointees because they're always treated as routine. It was probably something only a driven reporter like Judd would find. I mean he always saw things off the reservation. He had spent time in New Orleans, Joan Chatrier was from New Orleans, and he noticed something. I think it's that simple. Proving it now might be difficult, but I think he found something that made his trip to see Mari Roland logical and necessary."

"You mean like Joan was an illegitimate child?"

She laughed, but not at anything funny. "No, Silly, more like something we didn't already know," she said, giving away that she was still annoyed with him. "I don't know what it was . . . or is. I just think Judd found something and went to the source to test it out."

She could have sworn that Gordon snickered.

"And Joan's mother killed him to keep it from coming out?" he said.

"Could be." She was undeterred. "Have you read any of the blogs?"

"No, what do they have to add to the picture?"

"That you and the White House had him killed."

"To silence him?"

Kate nodded, unable to keep the smile from appearing on her lips.

This sounded to Gordon like a takeoff on the rumors that the President had manipulated all this movement on the court with help from her chief of staff and the FBI. "They have an overactive imagination," he said. "Is that what your brilliant Chicago police woman thinks?"

"I haven't pursued that particular point with her," Kate answered, giving him a little of his own back.

"Well, I wouldn't." Gordon said.

She placed both hands on her hips. "Gordon Cox, sometimes you go too far. Why shouldn't I explore the subject with her?"

He took a deep breath. "Because, my love, it will look like it's coming from the White House."

"That's a stretch, isn't it?" she said, and then cooled off. "Yeah, okay, I'll be careful. I know you're vulnerable on this, but you don't mind me peeking in up there, do you?"

"No, but be careful."

"Damn it. When have I not been careful? I only let it hang out when I'm talking with you."

"All right, so tell me again," he said. "What do you think I should tell Charles Black?"

Byron Colder, the writer Gordon had introduced to Joan Chatrier on behalf of his magazine publisher friend, Bernard, put the finishing touches on his notes covering the early segments of Joan's life on the New Orleans estate of Louisiana statesman, Jacques Talleyrand. Colder choked up the silk tie that he'd loosened earlier, put back on the coat that looked less used than the pants of his seersucker suit, and took out the comb he kept in the handkerchief pocket to manage his unruly locks. He had no use for a mirror when working with the comb since his hair never retained for more than a second or two whatever shape he produced when it was slick.

Colder had come to a fork in the road with some of the information he'd dug up in researching his story. He could run back to Gordon Cox with this info and risk cancellation of the assignment. Or, he might wait until the whole picture was out on the desk in front of him, write the story, and then burst forth in publication. He decided to wait. His ace in the hole was that both the White House and the new Supreme Court justice needed his work to be completely independent and free of manipulation. He'd play that card, if necessary, later to gain anymore time he might need.

The man was no stranger to the Internet and was very aware of the blog activity regarding the new Supreme Court justice. He didn't give most of what he'd seen much, if any, credence. In a sense the blogosphere was competition, and he was apt to be super critical of anything he read there.

The writer was determined not to divulge too much in the interview he'd scheduled with the Chicago police detective who was handling the case of the *Herald Tribune* reporter. It took him a few minutes to find the right office at the police precinct. When he met Julia Gold, he was surprised at her intelligence and pleasant appearance. If his story developed in the right direction, he'd include a picture of her with his article.

Julia didn't like the looks of the man. His cotton suit was wrinkled and spotted like he'd slept in it. The man himself seemed alert enough, but there was something untidy about him. Julia was attracted to cool and crisp. Colder seemed soft and soggy, like a bottom feeder. Too busy to do a background check on him before he reached her office, she assumed the worst, dialed in her most pleasant tones, and relied on her instincts.

"So, you're writing something on Justice Chatrier?" she said after Colder introduced himself. "She's an interesting person. I can't wait to read what you write, Mr. . . . ?"

"Colder, Byron Colder."

"But I don't see what this has to do with us."

He didn't answer the question. "Is it okay if I turn on my recorder? I'll erase anything you don't want to appear."

She hunched her shoulders, deciding she liked the man less and less. She intended to say nothing she wouldn't want repeated, and she gave him a slow nod.

Colder flipped the switch to record, and took out a large notepad and a pen from the scuffed briefcase he'd set on Julia's desk. "I believe you recovered the murder weapon in the case of the reporter who called on Justice Chatrier's mother."

"We haven't termed it a murder, Mr. Colder."

"But you found the reporter's blood on it."

"No comment."

"I read he was struck on the back of the head," Colder pressed.

This information had been released to the newspapers. "Yes," she answered. It was odd being the one answering the questions rather than asking them. She found it a bit like testifying in court, aware that she'd need to be equally careful in what she said.

"But you've found no connection between that instrument and Justice Chatrier's mother, Mrs. Roland?"

"No comment."

"All his identity was removed. I mean, the labels to his clothes and other items like a wallet and business cards."

The *Tribune* had run a story on that. "That's right," she said.

"Shoes?"

"No."

She watched Colder write furiously on his notepad.

"No DNA on anything?"

"None we could match. Not yet, anyway," she said.

"But he was otherwise fully dressed?"

"Well dressed," she said with a nod for emphasis.

"Was he killed where he was found?"

"We don't know that," Julia said.

"And there were no eyewitnesses?"

"No one has come forward."

"Could Mrs. Roland have dragged him from the house to the alley?"

"I'm not going to speculate, Mr. Colder."

Colder looked at her. "I see," he said, wiggling his torso and uncrossing and crossing his legs. "But there was quite a bit of speculation on the blogosphere around that time," Colder said in a voice that suddenly seemed shaky.

"I don't spend much time surfing the Internet, Mr. Colder," she said with a laugh. She knew of one case that had been solved by detectives surfing on the Web. Maybe she should take a spin.

"Yes, well, you did question Mrs. Roland on that?"

"I can't speak to that. We have an ongoing investigation here."

"I only thought the two must be somehow connected," Colder said, fidgeting.

"Maybe or maybe not," Julia shrugged.

"But you do know that Judd Arnold came here for the purpose of speaking with the justice's mother, and that he did, in fact, do that."

"No, I don't know that."

"Could his death be unrelated?"

Julia was getting tired of fending off the writer's fishing expeditions. "Why not? Where is it written that a young man traveling in this area of Chicago could not be accosted from behind by someone, robbed of the cash in his pocket, and left in the street to die?"

Colder tried again. "And the labels in his coat?"

"Not everything people do is rational, Mr. Colder."

"But the person must have known you'd eventually identify him."

"Perhaps."

"Play a game with me, Detective. Suppose there was another person who followed Judd Arnold and saw him enter Mrs. Roland's house. Then killed him to keep whatever Arnold had learned from his meeting with her from being disclosed?"

"I don't play games, Mr. Colder."

"But you've got to admit that's a possibility."

"No, I don't."

"But nothing you've found to date would rule out such a scenario."

"Nor rule out more than a few others."

Colder nodded, but he made no apology. "Do you have a theory as to what happened to Mr. Arnold?"

"I don't deal in theories too much; facts are better."

Colder continued to squirm in his seat. He appeared uncomfortable, but he pressed on. "No one is saying anything about why he came to this city. That's a red flag to me. It smells of cover-up."

She paused and smiled. "Are you a bull, Mr. Colder?"

Colder laughed. "You know what I mean." Then, he fell silent.

"Okay, Mr. Colder, if you're finished now, I have a couple of questions for you."

"Of course, Detective Gold. I'll help in any way I can. Before we start, may I use the facilities?"

As Colder left that day, Julia thought he'd be well advised to get rid of that light cotton seersucker suit. She also concluded that he knew much more about Roland's life in New Orleans than he'd volunteered. The man had been fishing, or maybe had he just needed to talk with someone who knew the person about which his story was based? His abrupt manner in addressing the issues was a warning to her. Since he came from D.C., she wondered if Kate Stevens would know anything about the man's involvement.

MOTHERS AND DAUGHTERS

Gordon was doing his usual, preparing dinner. Kate recognized the voice on the phone.

"Gordon, it's for you," she called. "On your phone here in the office." He couldn't pick that line up in the kitchen. "He'll be right here, Joan," Kate said, not waiting for a response. Then, when Gordon came across, she said quietly, "It's your favorite justice."

"Joan?" he asked.

Kate nodded.

"Hello?"

"I hope I'm not ruining your evening at home, Gordon."

"It's okay, Joan. What's up?"

"What's up? Are you kidding? Don't you read *The Washington Post?* My mother's about to be arrested, that's what's up."

"I heard . . . and I apologize for not contacting you, but Kate and I thought you might prefer it if we stayed out of it."

Kate saw the beauty of Gordon's excuse. By bringing her in on it, he made his action Joan's doing, not Kate's.

Gordon held up a tipping hand. Kate went into the kitchen, returning with a smile and the martini he'd left on the counter.

"How are you holding up?" Gordon asked Joan.

Kate handed Gordon his drink and sat down across from him on the ottoman to hear a sliver of what Joan Chatrier was saying. Gordon nodded his thanks to Kate and took a sip.

"The lawyer I hired to represent Mama in Chicago heard that the FBI was coming in on the case. I thought you might know something about it."

"Joan, I can't even discuss that with you. The White House chief of staff has asked for my advice on handling questions about this case, and that gives me a conflict, as if I didn't already have one."

"Do they want me to resign?"

"I haven't heard anyone say that, and I doubt it very much. Why should they?"

"Would I have been confirmed if this had broken earlier?"

"If what had been known—your mother talking to the police? What's so awful about that?"

"Would she have nominated me?"

"You are not your mother."

There was a long pause from Joan's end of the line. Kate watched Gordon finish his drink in one gulp.

"Mother has always been the tough one. She's so smart and clear thinking. She's gotten me through every difficult time I've had in my life. Now I need help dealing with her."

"I'm sorry, Joan, I can't play that role for you. Go get yourself some really good advice. Is anyone handling this for your mother?"

"I persuaded John Wilkins to take it, but Mother won't talk with him."

"She'll talk with you, won't she?"

"Not about the case. She refuses."

"Why?"

"You don't want to hear my answer to that."

"She doesn't want to involve you."

"Yes, that's right, but I care more about her than I do myself or any damn Supreme Court."

"So tell her, if she doesn't let you help, you'll resign."

"You know how I feel about bluffs."

"Who said anything about a bluff? Does your mother know you don't bluff?"

"Oh, yes, she knows. She is the person who taught me that little lawyer's gem."

"Then tell her either she lets you or Wilkins help her or you're going to quit the court, and mean it. Explain to her that, otherwise, you lose control of the whole situation, and that's not acceptable for you."

Silence greeted Gordon from the other end of the connection, and he waited patiently for Joan to come back to him.

"Gordon?" she said after a few moments.

"Yes."

"Do you know John Wilkins?"

"Not really. I've met him at Bar Association gatherings, but that's about it. He has a very good rep."

"I'm not sure he's the type to get in close with Mother. He'll do a great job in court, but right now I need something different."

"I can't do it, Joan."

"Maybe you can think about who else might."

"Someone better than her daughter," he said, "one of the best damn trial lawyers in the country? No, I can't."

"Mothers and daughters—you don't know much about that, do you?"

Gordon thought that was a cheap shot. He knew about Kate and her mother, didn't he?

Chatrier paused for a moment before saying, "All right, I'll give it a try. May I call you again?"

"Sure, but I can't cross the line. You've got to assume that anything you tell me cannot be privileged."

"I'll try not to compromise either of us."

Kate sat wide-eyed on the ottoman. "Whoa, that was a narrow escape."

"Think so?" he said.

"Talk about wiggle room . . ."

"She'll handle it okay," Gordon said. "She's a very resourceful person. It's the mother I worry about." Gordon gazed fondly at Kate, reached out, and took her hand. "Come and keep me company in the kitchen while I finish our casserole."

108ᵀᴴ STREET, CHICAGO, ILLINOIS

It was after nine in the evening when Joan Chatrier's rented car, her Protective Service officer behind the wheel, pulled up in front of the house on 108ᵗʰ Street on Chicago's Southside. The street was in semi-darkness, and the living room was dark.

The agent got out of the car and helped Joan with her overnight bag. The expression on his face evidenced an alert apprehension for being in this location at this hour of the night. The officer accompanied her to the front door, and stood looking around as Joan rang the doorbell. They waited for several minutes.

"Do you have a key?" the agent asked.

"No," Joan answered, and tried the door latch.

The door swung open revealing a dark entry hall and no lights.

"She sleeps upstairs. She's probably taking a nap. You wait here, Thomas, and I'll roust her out."

Charier found the hall light switch, and climbed up the steep stairway. The boards creaked under her weight, but she heard no sound coming from her mother's bedroom.

133

The call got Gordon out of bed. Kate rolled over as he took his private phone into the kitchen. The voice on the other end of the connection spoke in a hoarse whisper.

"Hello? You'll have to speak up," he said.

"She's dead, Gordon."

"I still can't hear you," he said. "Can you speak up a little? Who is this?"

"It's Joan, Gordon. Mother killed herself tonight."

"Joan? Where are you?"

She raised her voice a decibel, but it was like static crackling at him. "I took your damned advice. She agreed to go through everything. It worked . . . my threatening to resign from the court. She knew I'd do it. So, she killed herself . . . took a whole bottle of sleeping pills."

He said nothing. He could hear the sound of his own breathing. "My God, Joan, I didn't think she'd do anything like that." Why did he feel like it was his fault? Joan left no doubt how she felt.

"Gordon Cox, I'll never forgive you . . . you and your goddamned friend, the President. But I need to deal with this now. It'll be in all the papers the moment I start calling around."

Gordon knew she was right about that. "Where's your Protective Service agent now?"

"He's out in the car. He'll be back any minute. I need to do something."

"Why not have Wilkins handle it?"

"Then who's the defendant? Mother or me?"

"Good point. What can I do?"

"I want you to call that detective at the Chicago P.D., the one who's been hounding mother, and tell her what happened. It's the least you can do, Gordon. You owe me that."

He didn't answer right away. He was stretched out between his loyalties to the President and feeling guilty as charged. His mind soared through the possibilities like a world-class chess player would envision his opponent's moves. Only this was multidimensional chess. The toughest question was who was the opponent?

"Okay," he said. "We both know you can't leave there without calling the police. And I would agree, the person to call is Detective . . . what's her name? Gold. Kate has had dealings with her," he continued. "Can you wait ten minutes while I speak with Kate?"

"What will she tell the police?"

"She'll tell Gold what you've just told me, and she'll ask for restraint in handling the matter until you can make a quiet, smooth withdrawal."

"Okay, but will Kate do it?"

"I'll ask her, but keep the scene clean. And don't let your protection agent into the house. You don't need that complication."

A MEASURED MILE

Kate called Julia Gold at the cell phone number the detective had provided in case of an urgent development. Kate doubted she'd meant anything like this, but Julia answered on the second ring.

"This is Gold."

"Detective, this is Kate Stevens . . . from Washington?"

"Oh, Kate. Hey, what's happening?"

"I have a little bomb to drop on you, Detective Gold, and I'm hoping for a favor."

If Julia Gold's father could see her now, he'd know his careful coaching had born fruit. All of Julia's alarms went off at once: an involved person, bright, a lawyer, Supreme Court law clerk, beautiful, sexy, a friend of the victim, and a fiancée who was tight with the White House, she was calling to drop a bomb and ask a favor . . . "look out, Julia," her antennae vibrated.

"Detective, are you there?" Kate said.

"I'm here. What's this little bomb you want to drop?"

Kate sucked in her breath and drew on some nerve. "Justice Chatrier's mother died today . . . an apparent suicide."

"When?" was all she managed. "Okay, that's the bomb, so what's the favor?"

"Justice Chatrier is at the Roland house right now. She's reporting her mother's death."

"What's the favor, Kate?"

"She will stay put in the house and keep her Protective Services agent out until you arrive and take her statement about what she knows. The favor is, you allow her to return to D.C. with the agent before news of her mother's death reaches the media."

Julia leaned back in her chair. She'd need the chief's permission to do that.

"Can you hold?" She ran into her bedroom to the landline.

"I can't authorize that," the chief told her.

If their roles had been reversed, Julia didn't think she'd give any such approval. There was too much that could go wrong, and the Chicago media would never forgive them. But she wanted unbridled cooperation from Justice Chartier, and she wanted to be free of dealing through some lawyer, who would hide all the evidence. She was willing to bet on Kate Stevens and a sitting justice of the Supreme Court. Both would know the right path to take and have little to lose from taking it. "Chief, just a few days ago, you told me how important it was for me to realize a Supreme Court justice must be handled differently. That's what I'm asking now. In return, we will have full access to the truth."

"Are you so sure?"

She paused and smiled. "Forget I used the 'T' word, but what do we have to lose? We go out there right now, interview the justice, and scope the scene from top to bottom . . . God, I've wanted to get inside that house for months. This is our chance. We take Mrs. Roland to the lab, and we let it all hang out from there. It's a no lose situation, Chief. Where is a Supreme Court justice going to hide? Besides, she's got the usual Protection Services agent with her. Please, Sir."

"Who are you going to take with you?"

"Whoever's on duty. How about Barn Wilson?"

"All right, Gold, maybe we can get that monkey off your back."

She returned to the phone and said to Kate, "I'm on my way, but I've got one condition."

"Yes, what's that?" Kate said.

"That you stay in contact with me on your cell phone every step of the way. Call her now and tell her I'm coming. Then, call me back and have your cell phone plugged in."

"Sure, I can do that, but . . ."

"But, what?"

"Remember, the justice has a Protective Service agent with her."

"You said she'd keep him outside."

"Yes."

"Okay, here's the deal. I want to be in contact with you every minute until I'm finished and I let you go. I want you there on your cell phone," and she repeated, "every step of the way."

"Sure, that's fine with me . . . and Detective?"

"Yes?"

"There's no game here. I'm doing this with my fiancé's agreement and at Justice Chatrier's request. Gordon's probably going to fill in the White House, but not until you tell me that it's all right, sort of a tit for tat. Also, I need to emphasize that Justice Chatrier approved this line of action. It was her request that I call you."

Julia Gold hunched her shoulders and let out a breath of air. "Okay, thanks for that. The most important thing you've just told me, Kate, is that this is no game. Now, keep that cell phone open, and don't depend on your batteries. This may take a while. I'm on my way."

This is surreal, Julia said to herself, driving alongside the elevated rail through the Southside on her way to interview a justice of the Supreme Court in a suspicious death case. If she starts representing her mother, like she was her lawyer, look out. Don't argue, and don't lose your temper. Your job is to assemble the facts, and you need to be patient, focused, and ruthless in that effort.

Julia stopped her car alongside the government agent, smiled, and motioned for him to meet her out of the car on the street. She could see Joan Chatrier watching them through the front window of her mother's house.

Thomas nodded, carefully opened the driver's door, and they stood between the two vehicles.

"I have been in Justice Chatrier's presence most of the time since we arrived. The justice told me what happened, Officer," he said.

"Okay, stay here, please, and do not inform any person of what we think might have happened here. If you do, I'll have no alternative but to take the justice in for questioning."

Agent Thomas nodded assurance. Julia drove the police car around to the back alleyway, near where Judd Arnold's body had been found months before. She and her fellow detective entered the house from the back kitchen door.

"Just so you know, Detective," Joan Chatrier began as they walked into the living room, "everything is exactly the way I found it when I got here."

Julia nodded, took a look around the room, and sent her companion off with a nod to inspect the rest of the house.

"We can sit over by the piano, Detective," Chatrier said.

When they were settled, Julia took out her recorder and began. "Do I have this right, Justice Chatrier? You came out here to confront your mother and talk about why she was being questioned by us and what actually happened."

"That's right."

"And you found her dead upstairs, where she is now?"

"Yes."

"Why do you think she committed suicide?"

"I assumed that she did. I can't say I really believe it. There was an empty bottle of sleeping pills and a glass on the floor next to her bed. What am I supposed to think? Maybe you'll find she was murdered or died of natural causes. All I know is she's dead, and as of right now, Detective, I'm blaming you and the pressure you've put my mother under for weeks for something she never did."

Julia took her comment in stride. She knew it gave her an opening, and she used it. "Why do you say that, Justice Chatrier? What is it she didn't do?"

Joan realized she'd opened the door to something that could only be bad. "I'm sorry, Detective, but I'm tired and upset. I came out here to give my mother some comfort, but I was too late. I don't really know what it was she was being accused of doing."

Julia did not let it go. "There were no accusations coming out my department, Justice Chatrier . . . just some unanswered questions. We have a witness who saw a man about Judd Arnold's age and general description . . . that's the name of the young man who died here . . . entering this house. Your mother said that never happened. Yet, Arnold was found dead out back. Was that what you were going to discuss with your mother?"

"I didn't know about any of that. I knew that you'd brought her in for questioning and that she was very upset. I wanted to find out what was going on, and offer my support."

"Did your mother leave you a note?"

"I didn't see one."

"Don't you find it strange, Justice Chatrier? Your mother calls you every day, month after month and she kills herself without so much as goodbye?"

Anger was called in to overcome the impulse to cry out. Anger over anguish. "That was entirely uncalled for, Detective Gold," Joan said. "Who do you think you're dealing with here? Suicide is not an everyday event. Why should any of the rest be normal and usual?"

Julia did not apologize. She wasn't sure she believed her. "You mentioned murder and natural cause as possibilities. Can you think of anyone who would want to hurt your mother?"

Chatrier looked carefully at Julia. Eyebrows raised, she peered over her nose, reminding Julia of a teacher in elementary school.

"My mother had no enemies that I know of, Detective, and she was not seriously ill. Does that answer your question?"

Julia did not respond. Instead, she asked another question. "Was the protective agent with you when you found her?"

"No, he was down here by the front door. I told him to wait. Later, he went upstairs with me and checked her pulse to confirm what I'd discovered. I mean, that she had no pulse."

Julia caught the attention of the sergeant who'd come with her. "Barn, you can contact the crime lab now. Tell them to get out here on the double, and keep it low key. I don't want the press or anyone else getting wind of this. No fancy lights and no noise." She focused back on Chatrier while the sergeant went into the kitchen to make the call on his hip-phone.

"Did your mother know you were coming home this evening, Justice Chatrier?"

"Yes, we talked about it last night."

"What did you think your mother was hiding from you?"

"My mother didn't hide things from me, Detective. I wanted her to tell me exactly what you had asked her."

"And you couldn't have done that over the phone?"

"Of course, but I wanted to give her support, too. We talk on the phone every day, but sometimes you need to be able to hold tight the people you love, and give them comfort and support. I was too late as it turned out."

"What did your mother normally use as a protection device?"

"She kept a baseball bat near the front door. I don't think she had anything else."

Julia motioned to Barn Wilson, who'd reentered the room, but he was already halfway to the door. He took an old Louisville slugger out of the umbrella rack and placed it in a plastic bag.

"No one has handled that bat since you've been here, correct?"

"I certainly didn't."

"We'll check it for prints," she said, as another police car pulled into the driveway and two plain-clothed officers knocked at the rear door of the residence.

Julia went to the front door and signaled to Agent Thomas that the new arrival was part of her lab detachment. Then, she explained to Joan Chatrier. "Justice Chatrier, I have a warrant to search this house, and those two men, and Sergeant Wilson here, are going to inspect your mother. I hope it doesn't offend you, but my instructions are to treat your mother's home as a crime scene."

"Do what you need to do, Detective. How much longer will you need to keep me?"

"If you don't mind, I'd like to have a few more minutes with you, Madam Justice. And I need to ask you . . . where did your mother get those sleeping pills?"

"The bottle is still on the floor upstairs, but it's probably the one I gave her almost a year ago."

"It's your prescription, Madam Justice?"

"Yes."

"You gave her the bottle?"

"Last year when she told me she wasn't sleeping well."

"Did she ever threaten to kill herself?"

"Of course not."

"Why do you think she did?"

That question, coming suddenly as it did, opened a hairline crack in Joan's solid front. She wiped the tears running down her cheeks with a tissue, and cleared her throat. "I can speculate, Detective, as I'm sure you can as well, but the truth is I don't understand it. It's the last thing in this whole wide world I expected. I can speculate that the young man really did come here that day, and that Mama might have spoken with him. But I cannot believe that she harmed him or that she killed herself to avoid admitting she'd not been forthright about the visit. But it's complete speculation, and contrary to everything I know about my mother."

"You didn't have any voices in your head telling you not to give her all those pills?"

"No. That was a year ago, but I wish I had, Detective. I wish I had."

Julia asked a question that had been on her mind since the first day she'd laid eyes on Mari Roland. "You've been a very successful and well-known lawyer for some time, Madam Justice. Why did your mother live in a small house like this, and in this neighborhood?"

Joan nodded that this was a reasonable question . . . one for which she had no credible answer other than, "This is what she wanted. She'd lived here a long time. She didn't want to change her life."

Julia's dissatisfaction with Joan's answer came through the airwaves to Kate, and it bothered her, too. She'd had that anomaly on her mind since she saw the address in Joan's phone book. Thinking about it caused her to miss some of what was going on in the house in Chicago. When she tuned back in, Julia was on another subject.

"We're getting a transcript of the hearings on your confirmation to the court, Madam Justice, but is there anything more you'd like to tell me that might be relevant to this young man's visit?"

"If indeed he did visit, Detective. Please don't put words into my mouth. Anyway, nothing comes to mind."

Fair enough, Julia said to herself. Next on her list was another unusual facet in the life of the woman who lay dead upstairs.

"We obtained your mother's telephone records. The number she called every day at 4:00 p.m., is that your number?"

"She called me every day at five."

"Five, yes, Washington time, that's right. Except on that day and one or two others when she didn't call. You called her later that day around six. Do you recall any of those occasions?"

"Not specifically, but one of the things we were going to talk about tonight was why she didn't call me that day."

"Why did your mother call you at the same time every day?"

"Habit."

"Habit?"

"Yes."

Julia simply could not believe it. She could not get her arms around such behavior.

Kate laughed to herself because she'd thought the routine strange from the time Joan had asked her in chambers to be ready for her mother's call.

Julia proceeded to question this behavior. "Madam Justice, I have a mother and she calls me more than I would really like, but never at the same time each day. Don't you find it extraordinary . . . the same time over and over again for months on end?"

"Extraordinary or not, Detective, that was my mother and that's what she did. If I was not going to be available, I always made sure the call would be answered. It started when I was away in college, and we just never stopped doing it."

At length, Julia let both Justice Chatrier and the detective's phone mate, Kate Stevens, go. Thomas then drove the distraught Supreme Court justice to O'Hare for their return flight to Washington. The news media would have the opening story by the time Joan reached Washington.

AROUND THE CORNER

Kate hurried to unplug her phone so she could move around again. It rang a minute later from Detective Gold's squad car.

"What'd you think of that, Kate? It's so bizarre, it can't be made up."

"That was a very special relationship, Detective. My mother and I don't see the world remotely the same, but those two were like one person."

"It appears that Mrs. Roland's whole life was lived through her daughter."

Kate laughed. "She owned it. Joan Chatrier believed she owed everything she had in life to her mother."

"And the mother took her life when she couldn't help anymore?"

Kate's reaction came without thinking. "Or to do her one last favor."

This was the first time Julia had seen Kate's aggressive side. She saw the image of Kate on the tennis court. "What's your point?"

"Detective, forgive me, but I think Judd found something . . . probably a fact that would hurt Joan's career, even her confirmation by the Senate Committee."

"And the justice's mother killed him?"

"That would have given her motive."

"Do you think Justice Chatrier believes that?"

"I don't know what she believes, but I knew Judd Arnold, Detective, and he was not the type of person who would jump to conclusions or act on impulse. That just wasn't Judd. I'm sure he knocked on that woman's door. Whether she killed him or someone else did I can't say, but Judd's death was somehow connected to whatever he found. And that had to involve New Orleans."

"Did you ever meet Justice Chatrier's mother?"

"No, and I don't think Gordon ever met her either."

"She was a formidable figure."

"That wouldn't faze Judd."

"I'm not so sure of that," Julia said, thinking back to her first meeting with the woman.

"What's your next step?" Kate asked after a thoughtful pause.

"I've got to give my chief a full report, and we need the crime lab and forensics to work out a few things. Let me know if you come up with anymore bombs to drop, Kate."

"Okay," she said, laughing. "Are you sure you're up to that?"

Following her session with the justice, Julia decided to speak with the woman's biographer before turning in her report to the chief. Justice Chatrier's biographer was how he'd introduced himself, but she thought of him more as a tabloid writer. She reached him at the cell phone number he'd given her.

"Has your research, Mr. Colder, confirmed that Mrs. Roland came to this country from Martinique?"

"Sure she did. She was 21 years old when she landed in New Orleans."

"And she worked for a family there."

"Yes. One of the old French families. The patriarch was a U.S. senator back then, and they were well known and well connected . . . still are."

"And Joan Chatrier grew up there, according to her testimony at the Senate hearing."

Colder hesitated. He paid attention to words, because they were his profession. Gold had said, "according to her testimony," and to that he could answer, "Yes."

"Do you happen to know why and when Mrs. Roland moved to Chicago?" Julia was still troubled by Mari's "hiding out" on the Southside.

"No, but I know she lived in Evanston, working in a household there until her daughter finished college. I haven't located the people she worked for there. They were older, and probably long dead."

"When did Justice Chatrier go away to college, Mr. Colder?"

Colder leafed through his notebook for the answer. "1972."

"Have you spoken with the family in New Orleans?" Julia asked.

"I've tried, but the current patriarch has avoided me. In fact, I was told, in no uncertain terms, by some damn sheriff down there to stop badgering him if I knew what was good for me."

"Really?"

"Indeed, it was very real. The Talleyrands did not want to answer any questions concerning Mari Roland."

"Why?"

"I don't know. They seemed embarrassed, even angry I'd say, to have had any association with her."

Julia let that roll around in her head. "Is it possible that one of them is Joan Chatrier's father?"

"Is it possible? Yes, if they met in Martinique. Mari Roland must have been pregnant with her daughter when she arrived in the U.S. Mari was an attractive woman—an attribute she used to get what she wanted."

"For example," Julia prompted.

"Well, in addition to being pregnant when she arrived, she was several years older than any of the other eleven women in her group from Martinique. These women were given a thorough vetting before being sent off the New Orleans. Someone made a notable exception in Mari Roland's case."

"Have you found anything to show that she worked on the side in New Orleans?"

"I told you, when I started to get too close, the Talleyrands pulled down the curtain. But I don't think Talleyrand would have put up with that."

Julia knew that politicians often sent journalists and lawyers to dig up dirt on nominees or appointees for high government office whom they opposed. Was Judd Arnold on such a mission? Had he been followed and then cut down by those favoring her appointment, in order to keep dirty secrets from coming out? That might explain the killer's rationale to buy time by removing labels and other identifying indicia. But where had that task been accomplished if not in the Roland home? It was dark in that alley, and an extended use of a flashlight would certainly have been noticed. She wondered whether the FBI had done any work on that premise, or was the bureau in on an attempted cover up?

Julia added her own thoughts to the transcript of the recorded interview of Joan Chatrier. She wrote that she still believed that Judd Arnold had been killed in the Roland home. No evidence existed of another person being present, and that left only one conclusion . . . Mari Roland had hit him with the toy bat that the boy JJ had found, her motive to prevent him from publishing a story that would have ended her daughter's chances for the Supreme Court. How to prove that with both Mari Roland and Judd Arnold dead . . . that was another matter. What was it the reporter had found?

"Did you call the President?" Kate asked Gordon after she finished telling her story of what had gone down in Chicago between Julia Gold and Joan Chatrier.

"Not yet. I'll phone Charles in a bit. See how he wants to handle it. So she kept you on the phone the whole time?"

"Yes. It was weird. I could hear some of the stuff that was going on. It depended on which way Gold was facing. I think Joan told her as little as she could without misleading or withholding critical information. The detective handled it well. She knew she was talking to a brilliant lawyer who knew what not to say."

"Did Joan know you were listening in?"

"God, I hope not."

"Could be a problem. Why did Gold want you on the line?"

"I assumed it was to keep me busy, so I couldn't tell anyone what was happening. She doesn't leave much to chance."

"What does the detective think about Joan's involvement?"

"She told me she thought Joan was holding back on what her mother said, and Joan's own opinion of why her mother killed herself."

"That troubles you too, doesn't it?" Gordon said.

Kate nodded. "Yes, it does. Mari's suicide was for a reason . . . most probably to hide something . . . to take something to her grave. Nothing else makes any sense. Certainly, Joan has figured that out."

The search of Joan's mother's home turned up no evidence that Judd Arnold, or anyone else besides Joan Chatrier and her agent, had been there. Julia looked through a box full of Mari's personal effects. There were love letters from various admirers, and a faded photo from the newspaper in Fort de France featuring a girl dancing in a street party with a man dressed in fatigues. The baseball bat contained no traces of blood, or anything else related to Judd Arnold—only Mrs. Roland's fingerprints, and those were on the fat end, not where hands were needed to swing the bat.

A coroner's hearing was scheduled in Chicago to determine the cause of Mrs. Roland's death, whether a probable suicide, an accident, or "other cause." Justice Joan Chatrier and Kate were each subpoenaed to testify, along with Detective Gold and the usual list of crime lab and homicide officers.

FRIENDS AND PRESIDENTS

The President was dressed for a meeting with the British prime minister. Gordon's thought as he entered the Oval Office with Charles Black was that she looked primed for that occasion.

"Good morning, Gordon. Thanks for coming over here so early."

"My pleasure, Madam President, and you look smashing. What's the occasion?"

"The British are coming."

"Of course, today's the big day."

"I guess it could be, Gordon, but I did want to speak with you about Justice Chatrier before these meetings get underway. What's the story? Does anyone know?"

"There's little doubt but that her mother's death was self-inflicted and purposeful."

"Why'd she do it?"

"Well, if she did meet with Judd Arnold it could have been something relevant to Joan's qualifications. We may never know, since the only two people who could have known are no longer with us."

"When's this coroner's hearing?"

"In three weeks."

"Are you going to be there?"

"Kate's been subpoenaed to attend."

The President leaned back, looked at the vaulted ceiling over the oval, and hummed a few bars of "Amazing Grace." "Should I have anyone at that hearing?" she asked after a moment.

Gordon didn't hesitate. "That's not a good idea, Rebecca. Your office's presence, anyone there representing you, makes it bigger than it is. Don't do it. The press would have a field day."

"I agree," she said. "Charles, do you?"

"Most definitely, Madam President."

"All right then, but what is Joan Chatrier going to do if this all turns out badly for her? I mean, what's the worst for her, and God knows for us, too?"

"I think that's already happened as far as Joan is concerned," Gordon said. "Her mother's dead." Then he lifted both hands as if facing a revelation. "She asked me whether she should resign."

"What did you tell her?"

"I asked her why she would think so."

The President beamed with humor. "The old question to a question routine. Do you lawyers learn that in school, or does it come naturally?"

Gordon laughed. "It was a serious question. Did she know of any reason why she should resign?"

"Oh, I get it. You asked her to come clean."

"The press isn't giving it much coverage, but the blogosphere is having a ball. There's a lot of speculation out there," Charles Black said.

"What's the consensus?" the President asked with a nod in the direction of her chief of staff.

Black took a piece of paper from his pocket that contained several scribbled notes. "It's pretty much split between being much ado about nothing and demanding her resignation for misleading Congress. Then there's the really far out stuff . . . everything from theories of stolen identity to the FBI having the reporter and maybe Mrs. Roland killed to keep whatever he discovered from coming out."

"Any of the blogs credible or backed up by facts?"

"Not really."

The President reflected for a moment, and time seemed to stand still. She looked at Gordon. "It's funny, but I was just thinking about my conversation with Chatrier here in the office. I remember telling her that her mother must be really something to have brought her this far as a single immigrant parent. Now it appears that was a dramatic understatement."

Gordon said nothing, but he was looking guilt in the face. He had known how close Joan was to her mother. He also did not comprehend why Mrs. Roland refused to move out of the Southside, but had not pressed Joan for an answer. Maybe it wouldn't have brought any of this to light, but he felt guilty for not pursuing it.

"All right," the President said, ending the meeting. "I've got to get ready for the Brits. But promise me, both of you, that you'll stay on top of this so we don't get blindsided."

"Got a minute, Gordon?" Black asked as they left the Oval Office together. "I need a bit more advice."

They walked around to the chief's office, and Charles closed the door.

"I need to call Minturn today and give him an update, such as it is."

"Well, the suicide certainly changes things."

"What's the worst?" Black asked.

"The Chicago police have not ruled out that Joan caused her mother's death because the sleeping pills were her prescription."

"That would certainly end it with a bang," Black said. "What's the likelihood of another surprise?"

"I don't know, but we need to assume that Mrs. Roland intended to take some adverse fact to her grave, possibly the same fact that this reporter found. The hearing held by the coroner's office might bring something to light. They have the murder weapon, but there's nothing connecting it to Mrs. Roland."

"So we just sit tight?"

Gordon nodded. "But prepare for the worst."

"Kate, this is Julia Gold. I need to know two things. Who is Byron Colder, and who put him on the scent?"

The message was left on her answering machine at home. Kate contacted the Chicago detective the next morning. "Byron Colder," she explained from what little she knew, "is a writer who has specialized in writing biographies of southern families and politicians. Justice Chatrier agreed for him to write a short biographical article on her life. I guess he was focusing on her New Orleans beginnings."

"Whose idea was it?"

"Colder's, I guess."

Julia had a hard time putting the Colder she'd met with a justice of the Supreme Court. "And the justice okayed it?"

"I believe she did. Why, is there a problem?"

"Colder was here a few weeks ago. He asked me a lot of questions about the Arnold case. I have to tell you, Kate, it seems to me this guy knows much more than he lets on. It was like he was writing a story with me in it . . . you know, the idiot cop who couldn't solve the case."

"He's an expert in southern lifestyles. His books have not been best sellers, but I hear they're pretty juicy."

That sounded more like the man she knew, but it still didn't make sense. "So why did he get permission to do this one?"

Kate chose not to acknowledge Gordon's involvement in working out the deal. "I don't think you could keep him from doing it. Perhaps, if Justice Chatrier cooperated, she could at least control some of it. She'd be concerned how her mother might be portrayed."

"I don't blame her. This guy is well on his way to making this story into a page-turner. I'm not sure presenting an accurate picture is his top priority, though."

That struck Kate as being funny. "So wait awhile and serve him with a subpoena to see what he finds."

"Ha, why didn't I think of that? Keep in touch on this if you hear anything, will you?"

Gordon called Kate at the usual time from LA. It was ten in the evening in Washington, and she'd just come out of the shower after working out in the gym.

"Gordon, your friend Byron has been stirring the pot."

"No friend of mine. What's he been up to?"

"Detective Gold suspects he's trying to turn her into one of his risqué southern exposés. She's certain he knows more than he's been willing to admit about Mari Roland."

"When did they meet?"

"Colder went to Chicago and interviewed her."

"What else did Gold tell you?"

"Only that Colder behaved like the Cheshire Cat, smiling inwardly and keeping what he had to himself while trying to pick Detective Gold's brain for all the angles. Should you give him a call?"

"Perhaps, when I get home."

"And when might that be?" she asked, rubbing the towel through her hair.

"One more day."

"Good. It's not the same around here without you. The word's out on the street, by the way, that I'll be leaving my clerkship. I received a call today from John's firm. Shall I go for an interview?"

Gordon paused. Here it comes, he thought. "No. Make old John wait 'til this situation with Joan blows over."

"Play hard to get, eh?"

"Of course. That's what you are . . . hard to get."

"How would you know?"

Gordon laughed. "They'll wait. And you don't want to do anything until this business with Judd Arnold is sorted out."

"I'll keep the gloves on. Hurry home, Gordon. I love you."

"I love you too, Kate." He could have added, "and I don't want to risk losing you," but he didn't.

BLOODLINES

Julia Gold knew the Judd Arnold murder and Mari Roland's suicide had placed Chief Donovan under a lot of pressure from the mayor's office. In reviewing all of the evidence, she'd turned up a couple of her own shortcomings. She needed to tell the chief about these before taking the action she had in mind.

"I went across the hall this afternoon, Chief, and spoke with the sergeant in burglary and grand theft. We spent some time going back over the record in the Arnold case."

Donovan listened without comment. Not a good sign in her mind.

"In the list of persons who were interviewed by homicide right after the body was found, was the name of an attendant at the Exxon station down the street from the alley."

"Can you move it along, Gold? I've had a tough day."

"Yes, Sir, but this might be important, and I need your permission . . ."

"What about this guy at the station?"

"This attendant reported he'd seen a man, quite tall, dressed oddly, and coatless despite the cold evening. The man came inside, bought a candy bar, and lingered for a time, watching an area up the street as though waiting for someone. The description of the tall man didn't fit anyone we had a sheet on, and I'm afraid we all dismissed the information earlier as unconnected."

"Who dismissed it?"

"I'm afraid I did, Sir. That's why I need your help."

"Go on."

"I drove out to that Exxon station two hours ago. The man behind the counter was not the person who'd been working that night, so I couldn't question him. However, when I stood looking out over the shelves of candy and potato chips, I was able to see all the way up the street toward Mrs. Roland's house. I should have gone over there before this. This stranger, on foot, with no car and no coat, was too out of place not to be up to something. I'm going to interview the other attendant this afternoon, and I'd like your permission to have our 'painter' work with him to draw up a likeness of the tall stranger. One of the other things we kind of let go on was the indication on Judd Arnold's body that suggested death by strangulation. The crime lab couldn't rule it out. That would have taken a man or, at least, another person. I've never thought just one person dragged that body out into the alley, either. So, I thought we needed to check out this tall stranger. I know it's a long shot."

"Weren't there security cameras installed around that store?"

"Yes, but some truck ran over the main cord. They've been out of commission since last fall."

"Well, we all make mistakes around here, Gold. I hope something comes of it. Go to it," he said.

The next morning, Julia had another idea borne out of desperation. Judd Arnold's European cell phone did not work in the U.S. No phone of his that did had ever turned up, though she'd done her best to locate one. And how had the Australian woman that knew Judd Arnold exchange text messages with him? Going back over her notes and reliving as much of the details about this killing as she could, a thought suddenly came to her. Was it possible that, as Kate Stevens thought, the call she'd picked up on the night before Arnold was killed might have been from her friend using some phone that had never turned up? They'd tried Kate's phone's memory, but it was not on her recent call list and Kate had not saved that number. She hadn't known it was Judd; why should she?

But, Julia thought, Judd's mother had given him an American Express card; maybe she'd also given him a smart phone. Ad Arnold had never volunteered that little gem, but Julia wondered if Judd's father even knew about the credit card. If he didn't, then his wife might not have wanted him to know about a phone either. She'd have arranged for it in New York, and it might have a number available to the NYPD. She gave it a fling, and this time got lucky.

The NYPD obtained for her the record of all Judd Arnold's calls on that cell phone. Julia kicked herself for not thinking about this link sooner. She focused on the time frame from April first through to Judd's death. One of the calls was indeed to Kate Stevens on the fifth of April, and a dozen or so to various persons in New Orleans. Thanks to the recent visit by writer Byron Colder, New Orleans blazed like a beacon on her horizon. Who had Judd Arnold called there? She dialed the several unlisted New Orleans numbers that the NYPD had been given by Arnold's service provider, finding little of relevant interest until she reached the last number, which he'd called more than once.

"Hello?" answered a voice that sounded strangely familiar . . . almost like a character in a movie.

One step at a time she coached herself. "I'd like to reserve a table for four at eight tomorrow evening," she said.

"We got no tables," the strangely familiar voice answered.

What was it with the sound of that voice? "So I don't make the same mistake again, can you . . ." The dial tone sounded as the person, whoever he was, hung up.

She dialed the number again and let it ring. She heard a faint "click," but no one spoke up.

She thought about something Colder had said. "The family that Mari Roland lived with is very well connected." If the name on that phone was the same, it might be reported to them, and she wanted to avoid tipping them off. She had an idea, and she called Byron Colder.

"The name of the family? Is that what you want?"

"That's it," she said.

"Talleyrand. May I ask why you want it?"

"My report to the chief. I didn't write it down when you told me."

"You've found something!"

"Thank you, Mr. Colder," she said, ignoring the comment as she hung up.

The phone book contained several Talleyrand listings, but none of the numbers matched the one Judd Arnold had called several times, the one she had just reached.

"Can you find out who owns a landline telephone number in New Orleans?" she asked an officer in the C.P.D. communications department.

"The FBI can get it for you," he said.

She knew the chief would not agree to expand the FBI's involvement. Then she thought about Kate. She obviously had connections in Washington, or at least her boyfriend did. She decided it was worth a try.

"Kate, I think your significant other might have a few Washington connections."

Kate held the telephone away from her ear. She ran into this type of remark around Washington more often than she liked. "Depends," she said, bringing the phone back into position.

"Fair enough," Julia said. "Thanks to your help, I've found that Judd Arnold called an unlisted telephone number in New Orleans while he was there. He called it more than once."

"In New Orleans?" she said, now keenly interested.

"Yes, but I have a problem. If this were an Illinois number, I could trace it without alerting the person or persons on the other end. I can't do that in Louisiana without risking the cat getting out of the bag."

"Does the FBI have it?"

"My chief doesn't want to use them. I need to make contact myself."

"What do you want Gordon to do?"

"Well, I had the impression that he was in tight with the White House, and that might be enough to get Homeland Security to help us out here."

"I can ask him. What's so important about this number?"

"To be honest, I don't know, but it was the only relevant number on Judd Arnold's cell phone other than yours."

"Oh, I get it. You think Judd was checking with sources in order to corroborate whatever it was he'd found . . . not just with Mari Roland."

"You got it."

"Gordon will call me tonight. I'll ask him."

A call from the White House came in as Kate emerged from her morning shower.

"This is Kate Stevens."

"Kate, this is Charlie Black. Got a minute?"

Kate laughed. "For you, Mr. Black? Yes, of course, I've got a minute."

"I need you to come over here if it's convenient."

"Now?"

"If it's convenient."

"To your office?"

"Please."

Energized, but naked, she said, "Give me thirty minutes."

She dressed in her best business suit and presented herself to an admiring, but suspicious, security guard at the White House. She was ushered in to the chief of staff's small meeting room through a cordon of security. A fresh appearing young woman gave her a cup of coffee, and she waited. Black arrived ten minutes later. During that time she watched staffers whistling back and forth in the corridors outside the room, bent on delivering the papers and files in their hands. One, whom Kate thought she recognized, looked in and gave her a smile.

Charles Black apologized for making her wait, and got right to it. "I guess you know that Gordon called me last night."

Great, she thought, and nodded.

"It's pretty early out there. He said that you started this Homeland Security business. That's what I called you about."

"Guilty as charged, Sir."

"Okay, so the person who has that number is a Mr. Philippe Talleyrand. Know him?"

"I've heard the last name."

"That's where Joan Chatrier grew up, isn't it?"

"Yes, if it's the same family."

"More than likely it is, Kate. What's this Chicago detective going to do with it?"

"She's still trying to find out who killed Judd, and he apparently called that number several times when he was in New Orleans. But I thought the name Detective Gold gave me was Jacques, not Philippe."

"This man is pretty young. They thought he was a boy," Black said.

Kate made a note.

"There's one more thing. Philippe Talleyrand might be retarded."

"How did . . ."

"He never attended school of any sort, and even today no one has seen him out of the house unattended."

She thought later of dozens of questions she should have asked, but all she could say on the moment was, "May I pass this on to Chicago?"

"Yes, but I don't . . . this office doesn't . . . want to be involved. So be very discreet."

Black was also given information about the rumor being pushed by the blogosphere, that Joan Chatrier had an illegitimate son, but his preference was not to pass on information he couldn't verify. Anyway, it couldn't be this man. He was almost Joan's age.

Julia agreed to keep Kate's confidence on the source of her information and thanked her. Then, she called Byron Colder.

"Philippe? Where did you come up with that name?" Colder asked, showing more surprise than Julia expected.

"Never mind, Mr. Colder. Just tell me if you know who he is."

The writer didn't answer at first, as if exploring his options. Perhaps realizing he didn't have any, he said in barely a whisper, "He's probably Justice Chatrier's half brother."

"Damn," she whispered, and then, "Do you know that for a fact?"

Byron Colder smelled blood. "Why has this come up? Is Talleyrand involved in all of this?"

"Don't go jumping to conclusions, Mr. Colder. I'm merely checking out all the people who've been contacted in order to put my report to bed."

"Who contacted him? None of them would speak with me."

"Don't get all excited here, Mr. Colder. I just wanted to see if you knew this guy."

But writer Colder knew a good story from a glimpse of one, and this information spurred him on, sending him back to New Orleans once more to look more closely into a Philippe Talleyrand's life around the time he crossed paths with Mari Roland.

IN AN ENGLISH GARDEN

Julia leaned back, looked at the ceiling, thanked her father, and let out a lung full of air. Judd Arnold may have found a half brother who'd been kept under wraps his entire life. Was this what Arnold had wanted Mrs. Roland to confirm? His birth date would make him barely younger than Joan Chatrier. Julia thought the justice must know she had a half brother.

To test the waters, the detective once again called her friend in D.C., but she was disappointed by Kate's reaction.

"I don't see this as the type of revelation that would appeal to Judd. He'd think this was a private matter to be left that way."

"Well, you knew the man, but I thought you might find out something for me."

She guessed another test for Gordon was coming. "What is it?"

"Does Justice Chatrier know she has a brother?"

"That will have to wait for Gordon. He's due back tomorrow morning from LA. Do you work on Saturdays?"

"Not tomorrow afternoon. The Cubs are in town. You can call me on Sunday."

"I will if . . . I'm not sure Gordon will want to ask her."

"Let me know either way. I'll make the contact myself on Monday if he doesn't prefer to do it. But I don't want to make it sound like a big deal."

Kate let Gordon sleep late. Her heart wasn't into waking him up. It was only eight o'clock in LA, and Gordon was wiped out by his red-eye flight

167

into D.C. Besides, she didn't believe Detective Gold was on to anything big with this half brother business.

"That was a great omelet, Kate. Where'd you learn to do that?"

"Mostly by accident, Gordon. There was a diner near the campus in Palo Alto that made omelets like that, only better."

Gordon savored the last bite and placed his fork on the empty plate. "That was very good. Now, what's this New Orleans business all about?"

She filled her coffee cup, and sat down next to him at the breakfast table.

"Julia Gold has an unknown male casing the Roland house on the night of Judd's murder. Joan, it turns out, has a brother named Philippe, who is a year or so younger than she."

Gordon's first reaction was to wonder why Joan hadn't told him she had a brother. He shook his head in mild disgust. "Making him early to mid-fifties," he said.

"Right. Do you think Joan knows about Philippe?"

"She's never mentioned him," Gordon said.

"So, if Joan doesn't know she has a brother, Mrs. Roland might have wanted to keep that fact a secret."

"Okay," Gordon said, "but was that enough for her to kill herself?"

"Would it make a difference if the brother was retarded?"

"Why?" Gordon said. "Joan's mother was a strong woman. I don't see a little embarrassment driving her to suicide."

"Wouldn't it have affected Joan's confirmation?"

"I doubt it."

"Not even if Joan had a retarded brother?" Kate could imagine how the press would play it.

"Joan isn't retarded."

"Okay," Kate said, still testing. "So it wouldn't affect the Senate vote. But would Joan's mother have known that?"

"Fair point, but she wasn't stupid."

"Will you ask Joan, anyway?"

"I guess I have to. This will come out sooner or later. The Chicago police are looking into it, and Bryon Colder will break the story if no one else does."

Gordon walked gingerly up the six brick steps to Joan Chatrier's front door. He was beginning to regret his role in what was playing out as a nightmare.

"Come in, Gordon." She frowned at the expression on his face. "You look dreadful."

"Rode in on the red-eye this morning," he said, shaking Joan's hand and letting her close the door behind him.

"Is this so important? Or are you headed back tomorrow?"

They walked silently side by side through the foyer and into the garden room.

"It's a good thing I made the coffee strong," Joan said. "Want something in it?"

"As a matter of fact . . ."

"A little bourbon?"

"Thanks, Joan. Maybe you'd better have one, too."

Joan studied him over her reading glasses. "You think?" she said, then went to the kitchen for the caffeine part of the drink.

"How about sitting outside, Gordon? It's nice out there on the terrace."

He followed, and took a swig of his doctored coffee before sitting across from his hostess on one of the summer chairs.

"What's up, Counselor?" she said. "I used to enjoy these visits from you. Now, I'm not so sure."

He took a deep breath. "This investigation in Chicago is turning up a lot of mischief. The Chicago police have uncovered a connection in New Orleans that you should know about."

Joan blinked, took a sip of her own brew, and waited for the other shoe to drop. If New Orleans was the clue, it promised to be unpleasant.

"They're focusing on several calls Judd Arnold made to someone in New Orleans."

Joan met his gaze over the rim of her coffee mug.

"The person at that number is a man named Philippe Talleyrand," he said, noting that his mention of that name brought no reaction beyond a curious squint as she sipped her coffee. He paused to be sure, then continued. "The police also have a man described as being underdressed for what was a cold night in Chicago, hanging around the area on the Southside, and apparently casing your mother's house."

Joan's eyes narrowed. God, how she wished her mother were still alive.

"Now," he said, taking a sip of his bourbon with coffee, "comes the difficult part."

The justice braced herself. She knew Gordon Cox didn't deal much in trivia, and accusations she could see coming that her mother had covered up facts from that night in April terrified her.

"They believe this man might have been Philippe Talleyrand."

"Are they . . . ." She stopped as Gordon raised his hand.

"And . . . that he may be your mother's son."

"Her what?"

"They believe, but cannot prove at this point, that he was born to your mother in New Orleans."

"Who is 'they'?"

He ignored her immediate question. He knew it was an annoyed reaction. He moved to conciliatory instead of defensively combatant. "I'm sorry to be dropping this on you, Joan, but it's going to come out and you need to know."

Joan gathered herself. "That would make him my brother. What did you say his name was, Philippe?"

"Yes, so you didn't know?"

"Good Lord, no, I didn't know."

"There's more."

She took a breath, and waited.

"Philippe Talleyrand apparently never attended public school, or any private school for that matter. He may have been tutored at home, but there's evidence he's somewhat retarded."

"Is he . . ." Joan stopped. The words wouldn't come.

He understood her question. "He's relatively light skinned."

"Like me." Joan leaned back in the chair, spilling her coffee in the process. She shook her head, and her eyes could have passed for those of a rattlesnake. She hurled the half full coffee mug hard against the brick siding of the house fifteen feet away. "I don't believe it. Damn it, I don't believe it. My mother would have told me a long time ago if I had a brother." Then she stopped for a moment, trying to brush the coffee stains from her blouse. "So who's supposed to be the father?"

Gordon hunched his shoulders, which, coupled with his expression, conveyed the message that he thought the answer was obvious.

"My mother and Talleyrand? No way. I can't accept that."

"Fair enough, Joan, but others are going to go there. Just be ready."

"Okay, I guess I should thank you for the heads-up, but Gordon, I . . ."

"Yes?"

"This came from the Chicago police? Is that who you said came up with this? Do the police think this is the reason my mother killed herself?"

"I don't think that's where they're going with it."

"Do they think maybe this man, Philippe, killed the reporter?" Joan paused, but never took her eyes off him. "What's going to happen next?"

"You . . . or I . . . need to tell the Chicago police that you weren't aware you had a brother. If you wish, I'll tell them for you."

Joan didn't answer right away. She stood, walked over to the smashed coffee mug, and gathered up the pieces. Then, she turned to face Gordon. "You can tell them that . . . yes, but also tell them that I'm still not aware I have a brother."

"As for what happens next . . . my guess is they'll try to bring Philippe in for questioning."

"If I know anything about justice in that part of the world, they'll have a fight on their hands if they try to lay a finger on one of the Talleyrands, even if he's half a Roland."

"You may be right, but that won't keep the media from speculating, and the pressure this brings could force the family's hand."

"Not from anything my mother ever told me."

He was walking on eggshells. "Joan, let me ask you something, and please don't shoot the messenger. Do you recall another child in the house when you were two or three . . . before you and your mother left?"

Joan walked back toward Cox, brushed a drop of coffee off the seat of her chair, and sat down. "Yes, I vaguely recall there was a baby, but wouldn't I have noticed the connection if Mama had been the mother?"

"Weren't you only one or two?"

"I wasn't that precocious, was I? He could have been at the opposite end of the manor house from the servants' quarters. I don't recall much from those days . . . blotted it all out, probably."

"Anything you want me to do?" he asked.

"I need to let this sink in a bit, but please tell everyone you discuss this with that I do not believe this would cause my mother to commit suicide. Now, if you don't mind, Gordon . . ."

Kate wanted an excuse to touch base with Julia Gold. "I'll call Detective Gold, Gordon. I can give her the message."

Gordon nodded. "Sure. Thanks."

She made the call. "The justice did not know she had a brother, Detective, and she wishes to tell you that she still doesn't know that for a fact. She doesn't want to do anything to impede your investigation, Detective, and will therefore keep this between the Chicago police and herself until you tell her it's all right to confront the Talleyrands in this regard, but she'd appreciate being kept informed of your progress. Do you have her number?"

"Yes, I have it, Kate. Thank you, and thank Justice Chatrier for me . . . and your man, Gordon, too."

"Anything else new?"

"I can't talk about it right now, Kate. I'll call you when I have anything that I'm allowed to release."

This was the first time Kate had the feeling that Julia Gold might be hot on the trail of something or someone. She felt disappointed to be kept in the dark, but excited at the same time with the possibility of a break in the case. She wondered if Joan Chatrier was deeper in the web of this mystery than anyone thought. Gordon didn't think so, but Kate wasn't so sure.

Julia's next stop was her chief's office.

"Where're you at, and where're you heading now, Gold?"

She cleared her throat. "That Exxon garage attendant I told you about thinks he could pick the man he saw two months ago out of a lineup. He said the guy acted really strange. We have the attendant working with the 'painter' right now to come up with a likeness."

"Be careful, Gold. That was too long ago for him to be accurate."

Julia nodded. "The justice doesn't believe she has a brother. We have no reason to doubt her, but we'd like to find out where this guy was on April sixth. To this point, we've made no contact with the man or his family in New Orleans."

"He's a suspect?"

"I'm hoping the painter's image will end up looking like this guy. I know it's a long shot, but he's all we have at this point. Officially, I've named him a person of interest. I have the feeling if we shake the tree, a little ripe fruit might fall out."

"You're colorful if nothing else, Gold." Donovan laughed. "Are they going to volunteer him for you to question?"

"The family's name is Talleyrand. They're one of the old French families down there. Very proud people, from what I've been told, and probably embarrassed concerning this member of the family."

"Why's that?"

"His mother is Mari Roland."

"I got it," Donovan said. "But they've taken good care of this man all these years."

"They're also politically connected, and they don't have a low profile in that part of the world."

"Okay, so have the DA's office give it a try."

NEW ORLEANS

"The boy's not all there," Sheriff Wallace of New Orleans said over the phone to a lawyer from the Chicago DA's office. "He didn't do anything. Hell, man, he couldn't even find Chicago on the map, let alone get up there and kill somebody."

"Sheriff Wallace, all we want to do is eliminate him as a suspect."

"Don't you think I know how line-ups work? I think you need to file your papers for extradition. I'm not getting into the middle of this."

Sheriff Wallace hung up the phone at his end, and immediately called Jacques Talleyrand.

"Back to square one," Julia said in Donovan's office. "The DA doesn't think we've got enough to go on. He doesn't want to file extradition papers."

"Do you really think this guy Philippe had something to do with Arnold's murder?"

"Chief, I don't know, but we don't have much else."

"What about the artist's sketch?"

"The likeness looks seventy not fifty."

"What's her excuse?"

"She says the gas station attendant insists that it's a good likeness, clearly an older man, balding in front, thin face, big eyes, and a mustache."

Donovan ran his tongue over his back teeth. "What's the man's daddy look like?"

"We have a few old pictures, but nothing within twenty years."

"What is he, a recluse?"

"Pretty much. They certainly don't like their pictures taken."

"Why not post the likeness you have on the Internet and with the *Times-Picayune* newspaper in New Orleans. See what falls out of that fruit tree you're always talking about."

"Who wants me?" Julia Gold asked the desk sergeant. She felt frustrated with her lack of progress on the Arnold case, but wished she hadn't sounded so abrupt.

The sergeant didn't seem to mind. "It's some guy from a newspaper in New Orleans . . . the *Times-Picky-something*."

Julia hastened back to her desk and picked up the phone. "This is Detective Gold."

"Detective, my name is Douglas. I'm with *The Times-Picayune* in New Orleans. I've just been given the police drawing you all want published. May I ask why you picked New Orleans to publish it?"

"We've put it out in several places, Mr. Douglas."

"But why here?"

"I'm not sure I need to tell you that, Sir. Is there a problem?"

"Not a problem, but we have several people here who think they recognize the likeness."

She sat down. Got him!

"You still there, Detective Gold?"

"Yes, Sir, I'm still here. So, who is it?"

"This is not 100% you understand, but my editor doesn't really want to put this picture in the current edition. I'd like to make a deal with you instead."

"What's the deal, Mr. Douglas?"

"This is personal, Detective . . . you and me. *The Times* is not involved, okay?"

"What's the deal?"

"I tell you who I think it is, and you keep the paper out of it . . . me, too . . . keep me out of it, too, all right?"

"Who do you believe it resembles, Mr. Douglas?" she asked, meeting the newspaperman halfway.

"It looks a lot like Mister Talleyrand."

"Philippe Talleyrand?"

"No, not Philippe. His father, Jacques."

Julia listened in on a polite call the Chicago district attorney's office made to the business number for Senator Jacques Talleyrand. The senator's response lacked surprise. He'd been expecting the call since being warned by his good friend, Sheriff Wallace. He was also well prepared, having spent time with his own attorneys discussing his position and options. His reaction to being identified near the scene of a homicide was along the lines of, "Why not have your people call my people."

In this case, all the "people" were lawyers, and, following days of negotiation, releases were exchanged, and Julia was presented the opportunity to interview Talleyrand at his home. The deal the DA made with Talleyrand's lawyers was the alternative to seeking immediate extradition of the man to Chicago. The Chicago DA gave up that right in exchange for Talleyrand's admission that he was, in fact, the person identified by the garage attendant, and his willingness to be interviewed at home and be questioned on the subject of why he was there and what he did or did not do.

The DA wanted to send someone else, but Chief Donovan insisted Julia be allowed to handle it. "Don't worry about Detective Gold," he told the police commissioner. "We think this guy Talleyrand might have done the actual killing. Maybe she bopped him on the head, but it's not one hundred percent that the blow is what killed him. Talleyrand, by his own admission, had the opportunity to stop his breathing with a pillow or by placing a plastic bag over his head while he was still unconscious from that hit on the head. Arnold had a boner on when we found him. That's one sign of death by strangulation. It didn't make sense before, but with Talleyrand in the picture it fits the smothering scenario. Detective work is what we do, Commissioner, and Gold's a good one. Besides, our lawyers already gave away too much. We should have him right here in one of our cute, little jail cells. Then, we'd find the truth."

Before the meeting ended, the commissioner had to step in between Donovan and the lawyer from the DA's office. The assistant DA made one last try. "His lawyers will be there with him. We don't want her to blow the case against Roland by trying too hard to nail Talleyrand as a conspirator."

"We got where we are in this case due to Detective Gold's work," Donovan countered. "Let her wrap it up. If we don't like what he says now, we can still file for extradition. That's the deal, isn't it?"

Julia had never visited New Orleans, before or after any hurricane. She'd always thought it would be a wonderful place to visit. It was after nine in the morning when she arrived at Sheriff Wallace's office.

"Mr. Talleyrand will see us at eleven o'clock," the sheriff said. "We might as well tour a bit of the city, Detective. Have you had breakfast?"

Julia loved the fragrance of garlic and other spices from luncheons in preparation that wafted through the air in the French Quarter. They ate a late breakfast that might have been the best ever. When she and Sheriff Wallace finished their roasted coffee, they had just enough time to make their appointment with the Talleyrand patriarch on his home court.

THE LION IN HIS DEN

The manor house could use a few touch-ups, Julia thought as they entered through a front door opened by a well-dressed servant.

"Please, come in," he said, recognizing the sheriff. "Mr. Talleyrand is expecting you. He's in the library. If you'll come this way, please."

It really is a library, Julia thought to herself, looking at the stairway on wheels and a dozen or more shelves filled with books from the floor to the high ceiling. In the center of the ceiling, she saw a large stained glass skylight with lines and pulleys that allowed it to be opened from ground zero.

A very good likeness of the police artist's sketch sat behind his desk when they entered the adjoining room. She reminded herself that she was there to find out who had killed Judd Arnold, not to give this man cover for what his lawyers had already told the Chicago DA.

Talleyrand rose up and walked around his desk to greet them both.

"Detective Gold, thank you for coming all this way to meet with us," he said. "And Sheriff Wallace, it's good to see you again."

Julia shook his hand and took one of the two seats arranged for them at the visiting side of a modern desk, which looked out of place in a room that reeked of Old World charm. She felt like she'd gone back in time.

Their host pulled a chord behind his shoulder as he said, "I've taken the liberty of having a small lunch set for us in the solar room . . . after we're finished here. Would you like anything now? A glass of water, or perhaps a cup of coffee?"

"No, thank you," she said. "I'm still working on the wonderful coffee Sheriff Wallace treated me to downtown."

Talleyrand smiled, and he nodded at Sheriff Wallace in a manner that made her think the breakfast had been on Senator Talleyrand. Then, he leaned back in his chair and raised his hands palms up in a gesture that said to her, "So, you're here," an invitation for her to begin.

"Thank you for agreeing to see me, Senator. Don't we need to wait for your lawyer? I was under the impression he wished to be here."

"Detective, my lawyers are very expensive. I'll call them in if I need them, and I've discussed everything with them already. Let's get on with it. How may I help you?"

"I only know one way to do my job, Sir. I hope you'll bear with me if I seem too direct."

Talleyrand nodded without enthusiasm.

"Our sole aim is to find out who killed Mr. Judd Arnold, a reporter employed by the *International Herald Tribune* in Paris." She paused, and Talleyrand nodded that he understood.

"We have evidence that Mr. Arnold visited the home of Mari Roland in Chicago late in the afternoon on April sixth, and he was found dead early the next morning in an alleyway running behind the houses in the neighborhood a short distance from her house. We have reason to believe he visited Mrs. Roland to corroborate some information he'd dug up on her daughter, Supreme Court Justice Joan Chatrier. This occurred after the President's appointment and a few days before Justice Chatrier actually appeared before the United States Senate Judiciary Committee for purposes of being confirmed to the Supreme Court."

Talleyrand ceased nodding as she continued, but she retained his polite attention.

"We believe that this reporter discovered something about the justice, something that was relevant, and possibly adverse, to her being confirmed by the Senate."

Talleyrand looked at the Sheriff and then back at her.

Standing, he spoke. "I'm very impressed, Detective, with your ability to get to the heart of a difficult matter in so few words. Truly, what you've just laid out was succinctly stated."

Talleyrand walked to a table at one side of the large room and picked up an envelope. "In this envelope," he said, holding it up, "there are a few hundred words which my lawyers and I believe are responsive and relevant to your investigation, but first we need to discuss a few technicalities."

Talleyrand turned to the Sheriff. "Mr. Wallace, would you mind waiting in the other room while Detective Gold and I get a few things out of the way? It should only take a minute or two, and Bea will get you something to go with your coffee."

Sheriff Wallace excused himself with a knowing glance at his host. Talleyrand returned to his seat behind the desk, and seemed to pause to collect his thoughts.

"Detective, let's say I was in Chicago and went to Mari's home on that day. Let's also say I went to the front door and knocked. Say I opened it myself when no one answered and I saw a young man on the floor, and Mari standing over him with a small bat in her hand. She hadn't seen or spoken with me in over forty-five years, but she just stood there, looking right through me and repeating over and over again, 'I didn't mean to hit that hard.' Say I checked and discovered the man had no pulse. Seemingly, she indeed had hit him too hard."

Julia had come to New Orleans convinced it was too convenient for him that Mari Roland was not around to dispute what he would say. He'd worked it out with his lawyers to admit to being an accessory after the fact, placing him in control of the facts, and avoiding the murder rap. That was the game they were playing, and she'd come to town to discover the missing ingredient . . . what was his motive for being there at all?

Jacques began to dispense with the conditional tense as he continued. "I poured her a shot of whiskey, and after a few minutes she started talking to me. It was as if no time had passed since the last time we saw each other. She said the man on the floor was a reporter, and he was doing a story on Joan."

"And he'd discovered what?"

Talleyrand shook his head as if to say, "Why don't you listen?"

"Mari told me that she steadfastly refused to admit anything to the reporter, as only that woman could, Detective, if you knew her the way I did. But when the reporter turned to leave, she panicked and lashed out, striking him at the back of his head. She thought she was buying time to figure out what to do, but she hit him too hard. Mari was very tall. Her reach gave her a lot of leverage." As he spoke, he extended his arms to demonstrate.

"What did the reporter discover?"

"The identity of Joan's father."

"Why was that so important?"

"To you and me . . . or to Mari?"

"To the Senate committee?"

"I don't know."

"Do you know the identity of Joan Chatrier's father?"

"No, I do not."

Julia raised her hand. "Okay, let's say this was a matter of concern to Mari Roland, and, of course, her daughter, but I don't see what difference it made to you, or why you'd make the trip to Chicago to warn her." In there somewhere was the motive she needed to drag out of him. "Are you Justice Chatrier's father?"

Talleyrand appeared to have expected that question. "No," he answered almost casually, "but Mari's daughter was about to come before the Senate Judiciary Committee," Jacques added with both hands raised palms up.

"I still don't get it," she said. "Why did you care?"

"Because I had an affair with Mari Roland over a protracted period. She was my employee, a live-in servant of the family. That and more would have come out, and my family would be dragged through the mud and our reputation ruined."

Gold recognized lawyer-speak when she heard it. She guessed Talleyrand had been well coached. She chose the moment to play one of the cards she'd brought with her . . . *Angels Lust,* she knew, was caused by blood rushing to the area, which, in turn, was often due to the body being suddenly deprived of oxygen. "Mr. Talleyrand, forensics will produce evidence that the immediate cause of Mr. Arnold's death was not from the blow to the back of his head, but rather to oxygen deprivation. In other words, to being smothered."

"The young man had no pulse when I bent over him."

She needed a motive to tie the two points together. "Why did you go to Chicago that day, Mr. Talleyrand?"

"I told you, Detective, to warn Mari. Of course, we both had an interest in this young man not publishing anything about Mari or her daughter. I hoped by warning Mari, we'd be able to avoid the problem altogether. She could be very persuasive, Detective, but she didn't handle surprises very well."

"So you made sure he didn't wake up."

"Detective Gold, I did not kill the man. I did not hit him, and . . . " Talleyrand paused to take a breath . . . "I did not deprive him of oxygen." He took a deeper breath, letting the air out slowly. "As far as I could see, Mari also did not smother him. But he certainly was dead when I felt for a pulse."

"Why did you need to cover it up? The man was dead. He wasn't going to tell anyone."

Talleyrand took a deep breath. "I don't think she intended to kill him, but she also did not want the fact of his dying in her house to be known. Calling the police and admitting to an act of manslaughter would not have been much better for her daughter when you started asking why she'd hit him."

"Or for you, Sir."

"That's true. That's why I helped her dispose of the body in the way we did."

"So, you helped her cover it up."

"I had a choice. I could have left and said nothing, gone to the police, or helped her try to cover things up."

Talleyrand paused long enough at this point to pour water from a pitcher on his desk and take a swallow. He cleared his throat, and continued. It was as if he was talking to a supreme being or persons who weren't there in the room with the two of them.

"She wanted to call her daughter, but I told her Joan would have to disclose the reporter's death and where it happened. She couldn't do it, and, frankly, I didn't want her to. The young man was already dead. It's not like we were plotting his murder."

Jacques Talleyrand paused for another sip of water. Julia told her chief later that he appeared exhausted and near the end of his rope.

"Look, I know this looks weak now, and please don't take offense, but we were on the Southside of Chicago, a place I've always pictured as a questionable neighborhood. I figured a mugging in the alley wouldn't cause more than a ripple. Could have been a mob hit."

Julia laughed to herself. Where was she? The session was taking an *Alice In Wonderland* turn. Did the man really believe what he was saying?

"We cut out all the labels in his clothes, and carried him into that alley. She insisted on buttoning up his coat, almost lovingly, like he was going to be cold if she didn't. She arranged his arms in repose, gave him a kiss on the forehead, and told him she was sorry she hit him so hard. It would have been better to leave him there curled up in his shorts like I wanted."

At that point Talleyrand stopped and raised both palms as seemed a habit with him to solicit understanding. "I know this could make me an accessory after the fact, which is why I need to make a deal with your district attorney."

Julia tried going around to the back door, hoping to pick up a speck of truth that might help her case. "What did you do with all the young man's possessions?"

"You mean what was in his pockets?

She nodded. "For starters."

"In the river."

"Didn't he have money on him?"

"Yes, several hundred dollars. I put it in the collection box."

"Where?"

"At the church at the bottom of the street."

"I can check that out."

"Please do."

"Didn't he have a briefcase and a cell phone?"

"I took the case. I didn't see any cell phone."

"What was in the brief case?"

"I never opened it . . . didn't want to know."

"His overcoat?"

"It was cold. I wore it home."

She started to ask, but he preempted her question.

"Both in the canal," he said.

"So you cleaned out the money and removed the labels?"

"Yes."

"Where are the shoes?"

Talleyrand paused, and meeting Julia's gaze, pointed out the window. "Below the levee."

"What about the bat you said she had in her hand?"

"Mari threw it into a garbage can around the corner. I guess that was a mistake."

Julia wrinkled her nose derisively. Then she asked the question she'd been hoarding since she'd learned the number of Judd Arnold's cell phone. "What made you think that Judd Arnold was going to Chicago to see Mari Roland?"

Jacques pursed his lips. "He told me that's what he was going to do."

"What did he tell you?"

"He called here on Philippe's number. We allow Philippe to have his own phone. It's an honor thing. We don't offer him to the public as being different from anyone else. But I keep a close watch on that phone. People are not always nice, Detective. My son gets calls that are pranks aimed at making him look foolish. I answer a second call coming in if I'm home. The reason I didn't pick up on yours was I saw it was from Chicago . . ."

Julia recalled the slight "click" she'd heard on that call.

"Two and two still make four in my mind, Detective. Anyway, when Arnold called the second time, I decided to find out who the caller was. I answered."

"Did he identify himself as a reporter?"

"Yes. He was quite polite and very professional. He said he knew of my connection to Mari. He told me he needed to verify some things about her children . . . facts that he'd found in his research. He was very careful not to accuse, but I knew he'd discovered Philippe when he said 'children' . . . plural. I had to warn her."

"Didn't the justice know she had a brother?"

Talleyrand stood, and his expression hardened. "Apparently not," he said.

"So you assumed that's what he'd found." Julia pushed.

The man seemed to relax again. "I didn't assume anything. I didn't have to. I wanted to keep my family out of the public eye. But I thought about it too long. That hesitation cost me a day or two, and he got there before me."

Julia blinked and then squinted.

"I know what you're thinking, Detective. Of course, it was a mistake for me to go to Chicago. I suppose I felt drawn to her, just as I had been from the moment she got off that plane from Martinique."

In her last trimester? Julia thought. Why did being late term pregnant turn some men on?

"The only good thing that ever came from our being together was Philippe. I even asked her that day in Chicago to return to New Orleans and help me care for him, but she wouldn't do it."

They were getting off the subject. Julia brought them back. "Tell me, Mr. Talleyrand, what's in that envelope?"

"An outline of what I've told you, typed up by my lawyers, leaving out a few things."

"And what are those things?"

"My name, address, and anything else that would identify me sufficiently to make it a written confession."

"And you'll supply that if we can bargain?"

"Yes, of course."

"Will you come to Chicago voluntarily?"

"My lawyers will meet again with your district attorney's office under suitable arrangements. In time, I will come."

She felt sick to her stomach. The dark French roasted coffee was stirring around. She did not believe Mari Roland alone had killed Judd Arnold . . . hit him maybe, but that was all. The vision that played in the theater of her mind had Jacques coming upon the scene after Arnold had been knocked out and convincing Mari that the only way out was to end the reporter's life while they had the chance. This was the role he'd always played for her. "I'm your man, Mari, I'll show you how to fix it," . . . a pillow over his head or a plastic bag held tight around his neck, and she couldn't blame the Angels for lusting after his body. Talleyrand had managed to hide behind Mari's suicide, and Julia had not been able to shake him loose.

"A clever man, Mr. Talleyrand," she said as she and Sheriff Wallace headed for the airport.

The sheriff nodded without commitment, but he didn't look surprised that Julia might be going home empty-handed.

LOOK AGAIN

Byron Colder and Julia Gold passed each other like ships in the night. As Julia boarded her return flight back to Chicago, Colder arrived from Washington at Louis Armstrong International Airport. He'd come to examine the hospital records of the Catholic Church to see what he could find on Philippe Talleyrand. He went to the Hall of Public Records, inspecting all of the indices he could think of for anything that would tie together the lives of Joan Chatrier and Philippe Talleyrand. He found Joan's registration in public school, but nothing for Philippe. He unearthed records of Joan's inoculations against small pox and other diseases, but he found nothing for Philippe. It was as if the man didn't exist.

He shelved his disappointment, still certain he was missing critical information about the Talleyrands that many years of writing about vintage southern families told him was there. Colder decided to search the records of the regional office of the Immigration Service in Baton Rouge to see if they kept their own records of births to immigrant women who'd entered the country on limited visas. Maybe a record of Philippe's birth would be there.

He came across the same write-up that Kate's friend at the State Department had reported much earlier. There was documentation of twelve women, identified by name, who were admitted to the country as part of that program. Coupled with this file by some conscientious bureaucrat, and completing the circle, were the arrival records from the airport files. He uncoupled those records and copied the others, but when he went to place them back the way he'd found them, he noticed that thirteen individuals had actually landed on that flight from Fort de France, Martinique, and all thirteen had cleared immigration. Had Joan's mother been the added person? After all, she'd been pregnant, and that might have required special permits. Had she even been part of the group? Colder rechecked the names on the program list, comparing those names to the ones recorded by immigration at the airport. Mari Roland was one of the twelve. So, who was the thirteenth?

Most of Bryon Colder's contacts on the story he was writing had been with Gordon Cox. He didn't feel comfortable calling Justice Chatrier directly. He certainly wasn't going to call the White House. But that sonofabitch Cox was a lawyer, and that made him pause. He decided to sit on what he'd found overnight. Viewed in the cold light of morning, it remained too good an opportunity to let pass.

"Mr. Cox, Byron Colder here."

"Hello, Mr. Colder. What's up?"

"Would you meet me at Union Station? I have something sort of important to speak with you about."

"Can we talk now?" Union Station was a twenty-minute taxi ride in traffic.

"I think this needs to be done in person."

"Can you come over to my office, then? I have a full schedule this morning."

"I'm heading to New York. I'm afraid you'll have to meet me at Union Station."

"What's so terribly urgent, Mr. Colder."

"It involves Joan Chatrier, but more than that it concerns you, Sir, and our esteemed President. I think you really need to meet me."

"When's your train?"

"Can you be there in an hour? I'll be by the bar in the rotunda. You know, where the old information booth used to be before they rebuilt the Station."

Before my time, he thought. "Okay, Mr. Colder, in one hour, but this had better be important."

"It is, Mr. Cox. Believe me, it is."

Gordon spotted Colder slouched in his wrinkled seersucker suit at a table within the circular bar under the high-ceiling rotunda of Union Station. He acknowledged the bad feeling he had about this meeting, and walked in a wide circle with all his antennae up and functioning, as if scanning the large marbled room for conspirators, spies, ghosts, and T.V. cameras. Colder's posture went from slouched to alpine erect when Cox surprised him from behind. "Good morning, Mr. Colder. A bit early for corn whiskey, isn't it?"

Colder recovered quickly. "Cox . . . hello there. Thanks for coming."

He moved to join him at his table, but Colder held up his hand, pointing toward empty pews in the large general seating area that was never much used. "Let's sit over there, Mr. Cox, if you don't mind."

Colder swallowed what was left of his whiskey in one gulp. Then, he led Gordon to one of the benches isolated in the middle of the rotunda.

"What's this all about?" Gordon asked, sensing nothing good was about to come his way.

"The information I have," Colder began, adjusting his glasses and straightening up, "will destroy Justice Chatrier, and it will be such a scandal as this President you are so keen on will ever see. I'm here to offer a solution."

His instincts were being proven out. "Better go on, Mr. Colder."

"Yes, well, I've been mulling over how this should best be handled. I don't want to hurt anyone, but if I give this to you it cannot be gratis. I will end up losing the best story I've ever come across and go back to writing a few lines every other week for some newspaper. If you, or someone you know, might be willing to reimburse me for all the work I've done to date, then I could just keep this part of the story to myself. It took me to the bowels of the earth to find it. I doubt anyone else will do that."

This was not the first time someone had tried to shake him down. "What's the story, Mr. Colder?" he said, relaxing his taut muscles and appearing to stifle a yawn.

Colder took up the challenge, and, in a whisper that cried out for attention, he said, "Mari Roland was one of thirteen people who came in from Martinique on a plane under the French domestic help program. The program was for twelve. Now get this, the thirteenth person was a three-month-old baby named Jeanine Roland. That baby went with Mari Roland to the home of the Talleyrands." Colder looked intensely at Gordon Cox, searching for a reaction.

Gordon hunched his shoulders, lips closed but teeth not clenched, and a steely twinkle remained in his eyes.

Perhaps Cox hadn't understood. "It seems pretty obvious that your Justice Joan Chatrier was not born in the United States, Mr. Cox. What's more, I could find no record of a Joan or a Jeanine Roland being naturalized as a United States citizen."

A poker-faced Cox disappointed him again. "And?"

Colder leaned back and studied Gordon. "What do you mean, 'and'? If she's not a citizen, then she can't sit on the court. It's all been a sham. She'll have to resign, and you and the President will need to answer to the nation why you tried to put an illegal alien on the Supreme Court of the United States."

"That's a bit dramatic, don't you think? Illegal alien?"

Colder couldn't believe his ears. Cox was not acting according to plan. "A bit dramatic? Is that what you said . . . dramatic?"

"You better read up on your Constitution, Mr. Colder. There's no citizenship requirement for the Supreme Court. If Joan's truly an alien that's certainly news, but it's nothing the President couldn't fix in a New York minute. So what's this solution you wish to tell me about?"

Colder sat frozen in his seat. He'd committed a serious felony by suggesting, if not proposing, a blackmail scheme to an agent of the President of the United States. Cox had not raised a stutter in reaction. Sitting beneath Gordon's penetrating eye contact, Colder was suddenly frightened. Cox must have known this all along. They must have fixed it, and made her a citizen. His mind raced for a way out of his dilemma, someway to take it all back, to start over again in a more innocent manner. He'd come on too bold.

Gordon waited, and when he thought the moment was right, he leaned over and said in a quiet, calm manner, "You've let the cat out of the bag, Mr. Colder. If, in fact, Joan is not a citizen, which I doubt very much, I admit there might be some damage control to manage, but unless you have something more to tell me, I'm going back to my office."

He stood, turning his back on Colder.

Gordon listened to the heels of his own shoes clicking on the marble floor of the rotunda as he walked straight out of Union Station. He felt certain that Byron Colder had not chosen the site as their meeting place because he was catching a train to New York . . . or anywhere else . . . but he controlled his curiosity and never looked back. He avoided the line for taxis, and walked across the labyrinth of roads servicing Union Station. He continued up the hill towards the Supreme Court and Capitol buildings without once looking over his shoulder.

What had he done? What was Colder going to do next? He could have bought more time by playing blackmail tag with the man, but he had not done that. He'd called the man's bluff, and Colder might already be on his way to the *Washington Post*. He knew he had to speak with Charles Black. The sooner the better.

DIFFUSION

Byron Colder would have loved Charles Black's reaction to the news.

"He thinks she's not a citizen? Holy shit!" Black said, his lower jaw bouncing off his more than ample chest. "Mother of God."

"It's possible she may not have been born here, Charles."

"And never naturalized?"

"Colder seems convinced she wasn't. Joan certainly thinks she was born here, and if she has a birth certificate along with supporting hospital records, why would she think she needed to be naturalized?"

Black shook his head in disbelief. "We're looking here, Gordon, at an illegal alien on the Supreme Court."

"According to Mr. Colder."

"What's that pain-in-the-butt going to do with it?"

"He made his pitch. That's one of the things about blackmail. It's basically a bluff, and I called him on it. We'd best be prepared, though. When he recovers from his disappointment, he might be ornery. Meanwhile, who can you have check it out?"

"Certainly not the FBI," Black said with more cynicism in his tone than Gordon recalled ever coming from the man. Black looked hard at Gordon and stuck out his chin. "Why in hell didn't the bureau discover this during her background check?"

"I don't know, but I reckon it's what Judd Arnold found. If the FBI agents or the Justice Department lawyers checked the birth certificate at all, beyond knowing she had to produce one to be admitted to the Bar, they would have found what they expected to find. There was no reason to doubt it was based on an actual birth. Why would they go beyond that?"

"But you're saying that Colder, and maybe that guy Arnold, too, found it?"

"Colder stumbled on it, because he was looking high and low to see where Philippe Talleyrand came from and to tie him in with Joan for his article. The reason Judd Arnold might have come across the same fact was his desire to write a less impersonal history on Joan than the one set out in her obituary at the *Times*. Kate thinks he would have wanted to make her look like the Phoenix that Joan really is. When the New York paper wrote that article, tipping her for the appointment, while he was still in New Orleans. It was Heaven-sent. He was right there on the spot, but he needed to know more about her early life to make her part of the story. He must have stumbled on it just like Colder."

"Why didn't Judd Arnold tell his editors at the *Trib* what he'd found?"

"We're getting a bit ahead of ourselves here, Charles. We don't know if it's true that's what Judd found. But if he did find this, it must have looked like the scoop every news journalist hopes to get at least once in a lifetime. He would have wanted to write the hard news story, too, and that had to include checking with the source. He couldn't ask permission from his people to go to Chicago without giving away what he'd found. He knew they'd send a seasoned reporter out of Washington or New York to handle the rest. So, he used his mother's Amex card and made the trip himself to confirm what he'd found."

Black paused for a moment, and scratched his chin. "You're right, we need to check it out. If not the bureau, then who should I have do it?" Black asked.

Gordon had been wrestling with the possibility of a cover up. He had a plan, but he did not want to broach it directly. "Why add another potential leak?"

It took Black a moment to get it. "You can't mean have Colder do it."

"He's already done it, hasn't he? We can ask him to give us the exact evidence he found and tell us where he found it. Then, we double-check it."

"But he's a blackmailer."

"If his facts don't check out, we can forget about it. If they do, we'll of course, have to own up, but it might give us time to manage some damage control. You know . . . have the President make her a citizen."

"The press would have fun with that."

"I'm sure Joan would resign immediately if the President wants her to."

"Maybe she'll have to, but that doesn't help us much."

"Exactly, it's better if she stays on the court. There's nothing yet to implicate her in any kind of a cover-up, or to make her any less attractive as a justice. The President can make her a citizen and conform to the general conception that Supreme Court justices should be such. She did it for that Swiss tennis player."

"But the Senate will impeach her."

"On what grounds?"

Black gave Gordon the look he reserved for certifiable nuts. "Maybe on the grounds that she's not a citizen?"

"But the Constitution says nothing about citizenship being required for the Supreme Court."

"You've got to be kidding, Gordon, since when?"

"Since forever. Granted no one would be confirmed if it was known they weren't a citizen, but technically it's not grounds for removal."

"She lied about it to the committee."

"Not if she didn't know."

"You're serious, aren't you?"

Gordon grasped the risks, but he saw no other choice. "I'm absolutely certain she believes she was born in New Orleans. I asked her more than once if she had any skeletons. She said no each time, and I don't think she'd lie to me or the President." But as Gordon said the words, he recalled the senator from New York asking Joan during the confirmation hearing if she'd been born in the U.S. This, in turn, raised the issue set forth by Brad Smyth that day on the train back from New York.

"What is it?" Black said, noticing the sudden change of expression in Gordon's eyes.

"I don't know, Charles. I need to check something."

"Can't you tell me?"

Gordon took a deep breath. "At one point, before the hearings on her confirmation started, Brad Smyth . . . you know who he is . . . suggested to me there was a problem with the papers Joan had filed for admission to the D.C. Bar. He had seen her Bar application, and the sequence of numbers didn't add up. You know how it works . . . if someone's trying to hide a period in their life, they fudge the sequence enough in their CV to blot it out. I know Brad was in New York that day because he joined me on the Metro Liner. Maybe that's why the senator from New York asked her point-blank if she was born in the United States."

"That's troublesome. Did you mention it to Joan?"

"I called Joan about it the next day, but she'd not kept a copy of the Bar application and sounded annoyed I'd even asked her. Sorry, but I need to check it out."

Black probed to get a feel of yet another potential issue. "It didn't come up at the Senate hearings, did it?"

"Only from the senator from New York. I remember the question because it seemed redundant and out of the blue. She and others had stated several times that she was born in New Orleans. He might have been fishing."

"Did Brad ever raise it again?"

"No."

"But . . . ."

"What, Gordon?"

"The Chicago police detective handling the case of Judd Arnold's death asked Kate for a sample Bar admission application. Kate sent her one."

"Why did the detective want it?"

"Never asked."

"Maybe you'd better."

"I'll ask Kate to call her."

"Don't let the cat out of the bag," Charles said with a touch of panic in his voice.

"Of course not. Kate will be careful."

What the President might think was always in the front of Charles Black's mind, and he harnessed Gordon to the task of advising her. "We'd better decide what we're going to tell her. You're suggesting we talk Joan out of resigning. That would be my choice. I don't think I could live through another Senate hearing right now."

"Okay . . . if it's true that she's not a citizen, which is worse, having her resign and be deported, or supporting her as an almost unanimously confirmed appointment, whose mother did something stupid a long time ago and paid the price for it just to keep her daughter's career intact?"

"I don't know, Gordon . . . scandals have a way of infecting everyone who's close by."

"I agree, there's not much upside, but the downside doesn't give much away."

"You'd need to talk Joan out of resigning."

"If she resigns, she gets disbarred and deported."

"And then there's the Congress. I can't imagine the Senate going along. The opposition will be out for blood."

"Some of them have almost as much to lose as the President."

"They may not see it that way. The most accepted notion in this damn city is to point your finger at the other guy. Let the press take off with that, and no one ever looks back at you."

"You need to take the initiative, Charles. Isolate those you don't trust or who want blood. This is a tragic story that will appeal to the world's imagination . . . a young black immigrant's mother learns in the days long before 9-11 that her daughter would be a citizen if she'd been born here, so she uses all her feminine wiles to have the records altered to suit. When it seems someone has finally discovered the truth, she kills herself, thinking she'll be taking the secret to her grave."

"You're in the wrong business, Gordon. You should be on Madison Avenue or in Hollywood. I hasten to point out that the question of an alien mother getting away with falsifying her child's birth record is not going to sit well these days in places like Texas, New Mexico, and Arizona. Besides, won't everyone assume she must have killed Arnold, too?"

He nodded. "But Joan's mother needs to be a victim, not a killer, or we're all in trouble."

"When are you going to speak with Colder?"

"First, I need to call Brad Smyth, and then I'll talk with Joan."

"All right, Gordon, let me know as soon as you have anything. I think this merits a call to my good buddy, Henry Minturn."

"I wouldn't do it yet, Charles. Let me see what's out there, and then we can talk with the President."

"We need to hurry. One more question. Is there any way we can bury this?"

"And spend the rest of your life paying ransom to Byron Colder?"

"Yeah, of course not. We better give the President the news. Are you ready?"

"Ready when you are, Charles. It's not the worst we've ever had to tell her."

"I'm not sure about that, Gordon."

Kate was stretched out on the big couch in their living room when Gordon came out from the bedroom in his casual at-home clothes. "What did the President say about your idea?"

"Not much at first. We went all around the horn again with her, and that brings you back to few choices and none of them good."

"But no one is going to think that non-citizens should be on the Supreme Court, regardless of what the Constitution does or doesn't state."

"But the President can cure that in a New York minute. The real question is whether this taints everyone involved with her being there as either incompetent or deceitful."

"So she went along with it?" Kate said, getting up from her repose.

Gordon nodded as he opened the refrigerator in the adjoining kitchen. "Joan Chatrier captured the imagination of the public more than any previous candidate for the court. That's a powerful incentive to keep her there. She did nothing wrong here. She's a victim, not the evildoer. The White House needs to make that case, but I think, and she came around, that it can be done. If it's handled right the President might even come out stronger than ever."

"So, what's the next step?" Kate asked, joining Gordon in the kitchen.

"I've got to confront Joan with the facts, see what she has to say, and, assuming no more surprises, make sure she stands firm. The President will release the story to the press and, in the same breath, make her a citizen. Then, we fight the battle in the political trenches."

"That's going to be fun," Kate said, a lot of white teeth showing.

"Yes," Gordon said as he laughed. "Now, what would you like with your steak? It can soak here in the sink while I call Joan."

ON THE CAPITOL BELTWAY

"Sorry, Gordon," Joan said, "I just got your message."

"No problem."

"What news from the executive suite?"

"You do pose problems, Madam Justice."

"What is it this time?"

"I hate this," he said.

"That sounds ominous. Can you give me a hint?"

"Not over the phone."

"Oh, come on, Gordon. Don't be so damn melodramatic. What is it?"

"We need to talk."

"I'm all ears."

"Not over the phone, Joan."

"Tomorrow's out. I'm scheduled to give a speech in Philadelphia in the evening."

"How are you traveling?"

"By car, arranged by the people I'm speaking before."

"Got room for a passenger?"

"Sure."

"When are you leaving?"

"Nine a.m."

"I'll be out on the street in front of my office, waiting for you. Make sure it has mafia windows."

"What are those?"

"Tinted glass and bullet proof."

"Serious?"

"Well, tinted glass, anyway."

The big black limo stopped in front of the entrance to Gordon's office building. The driver and ever-present Protective Services officer occupied the front two seats, and, while Gordon couldn't see her, the justice sat alone in the back.

He walked toward the vehicle. The officer emerged to open the back door on the curbside for him. Joan sat with a large notebook in her lap and a cup of coffee on the elaborate tray section next to her seat. Gordon took the jump seat facing her.

The two of them chatted for a few minutes for the benefit of the others, and then, as prearranged by Joan, they sealed the other two off from their conversation. Gordon got to the point as the big limo wound its way west on Massachusetts Avenue and headed for the inner beltway, north, toward I-95.

"Joan, do you remember me asking you about your application to the D.C. Bar?"

"Vaguely, but I don't recall the issue."

"You asked me who had raised questions about it."

"And you wouldn't tell me."

"That's right, but I will now. It was Bradley Smyth, one of the lawyers for the Judiciary Committee."

"Sure, I know Brad. What did he want?"

"He asked me, if you were really born in 1961, how you could graduate from high school in 1976 when you'd be just going on fifteen?"

"Was that on my application to the Bar?"

"That sequence, yes," he said. "Some of the things you reported doing and jobs that you had at various times made you seem a bit older than if you were born in '61."

"Why are you telling me this now?"

"Because there's reason to believe you were born earlier in Martinique," he said, and held his breath.

Joan's expression was that of a person who'd just realized she could speak fluently a foreign language that she'd never studied.

Gordon thought back to all the meetings they'd had. All discussions based on the fact that Joan had been born in New Orleans. He prayed now that Joan would say something like: "Oh, sure, but I got naturalized." But that's not what she said.

"Where . . . I mean, how did you come to that conclusion? What's going on here, Gordon?"

"That writer, Bryon Colder, says he has evidence that a young baby girl named Jeanine Roland came in on the same flight from Martinique as your mother." He waited for a reaction that didn't come. Joan was either stunned or playing poker. "This may also be what Judd Arnold discovered when he was doing the research on you in New Orleans. He may have gone to check it out with your mother before approaching his employer with the story."

"That I wasn't born here?"

"That you came in on the same visa with your mother in 1959."

"That's not possible."

"Colder brought it to my attention," he said.

"That's all very interesting, Gordon, but I do have a birth certificate. I used it to get a passport when I was in college in Puerto Rico, and I needed it to be admitted to the Bar . . . oh."

He watched as Joan made the connection with the question Brad Smyth had raised.

"Your mother might have managed that creation when she realized you'd automatically be a citizen if you were born here. The Talleyrands probably could have fixed it. That seems more likely now that we know your mother and Jacques . . . "

"No, Gordon, please don't say it." Joan recovered her breath. "It can't be. I would have known. I only saw her lie once in my life, and that wasn't to me. No, she wouldn't lie to me about that."

"It's in the records, Joan. Judd Arnold must have found it, too."

"And you think Mama had him killed?"

He raised both hands. "Whoa! I don't think any such thing, but it may be why she killed herself."

Joan bristled in defiance. "She's dead, Gordon. I'm not going to let anyone spoil the love she gave to me. I don't believe she would do something like that. I was born here, I have a birth certificate to prove it, and that's my position."

"Okay, you hang in there, but this other business is going to come out, sooner or later."

"Does she want me to resign?"

"No. In fact, she'll tell the world when this breaks that you never knew there was any issue here, and she's prepared to make you a citizen by executive decree."

"When is the story coming out?"

"Anytime now, but we'd like to control it."

"How're you going to do that?"

"We now have the specifics on Colder's facts. If they hold up unconditionally, we'll let Byron Colder go ahead and break the story . . . and we'll help him write it if I can talk him into that." He waited to see if Joan would see the reasoning in what he proposed.

"I don't care what that damn fool does. This thing has gotten way out of hand, and my mother's gone."

"Yes, but you're implicated now." His eyebrows were arched and his jaw set as he inhaled enough air through his nasal passages to fill his lungs. He took a quick look to see where they were on the beltway. He knocked on the glass separating them from the two men in the front seat, motioning them to turn on the intercom.

"You guys are familiar with the metro station in Bethesda up ahead just off the beltway," he said. "You can drop me off there."

REVERSE BLACKMAIL

Gordon and Charles Black met in the evening in one of the old administration building conference rooms over a good steak dinner brought over from the White House.

"So Joan is still insisting she was born here."

"Yes, but she's accepted having Colder break the citizenship story, which he will release day after tomorrow. We let him take the credit, and he plays by our rules."

"Why do we think he'll do that?"

"If he doesn't, he goes to jail for trying to blackmail the President."

"Okay, Gordon, what else do we think?"

"There's too much discrepancy in Joan's apparent age if you shine a bright light on it. If she was born in 1961, she'd have been five years old in '66, but the records Kate found, if you work them back from Evanston, Illinois to where they moved, made her seven."

"That's pretty revealing. How does Joan explain it?"

"She doesn't."

"Is this the discrepancy you think Brad Smyth stumbled upon?"

"I didn't present the issue to him that specifically."

"And neither of them were ever naturalized?"

"You might still have that checked, but why would Joan think she needed to?" Gordon said, making the obvious point.

"So that's the reason the mother killed herself, to take the secret to her grave?"

"That's the most promising theory."

"What did Colder say when you spoke with him?"

"I gave him a choice. He could do the story along the lines we want or I'd report him to the FBI."

"Sort of reverse blackmail," Black said with an ironic smile pasted across his face.

Gordon grimaced, then smiled and nodded. "He doesn't get prosecuted, and this story will make him a hero to his media brethren."

"How far along is he?"

"He's close to finished. He promised it will be as much about this unusual woman, who committed suicide, as about Joan herself. From Colder's baggy-eyed face and rumpled shirt, I'd say he's been working around the clock. You'd best get ready."

Black's special phone buzzed as he started to say something more. He turned to Gordon after listening to the President. "She's ready for us."

They took the inside route to Black's office in the White House and walked through to the Lincoln Room. The Oval Office would remain dark on this occasion.

"So she's two years older than we thought," the President said as they joined her. "How could she have not known?"

"I'm sure her mother managed to obscure that early on." Gordon said.

"I've thought about it . . . long and hard . . . and unless you two tell me there's another shoe to drop here, I want this woman to stay on the court. She'll make a fine justice, and we've spent too much of the nation's time and money getting her there to just dump her now." Turning to Charles Black, she said, "We need to speak with the chief justice to see how it will affect the court's credibility, among other things. I also want Henry Minturn to bounce it off a few more members of the Senate."

"The timing is important," Gordon said.

"I'll say the timing's important," the President said. "Have you seen this man Colder's article yet?"

"Not yet," Black said.

"What's Joan Chatrier's input going to be?" the President asked Cox.

"She'll look after her mother being portrayed too cynically."

"But you'll have a chance to tone it down, if necessary?"

"We don't want Colder to be able to say the White House edited it. He'll catch some criticism, too, and we don't want him to use Charles here as his scapegoat."

"Goodness, no." The President laughed. "That's my prerogative, and it's jealously guarded, too. Seriously though, Gordon, doesn't she need to resign? Aren't we just kidding ourselves here?"

That's what Kate thinks popped into his head, and he almost told the President that. Instead, he stayed with his game plan. "She can always do that, Rebecca, but I think you need to make the point that no one, not even Joan herself, knew about this, that she was your choice, and will be one hell of a good justice. It's gutsy and not without risk, but that's what the people have become accustomed from you."

"Is 'gutsy' what's going to be on my tombstone?" the President asked, looking to her chief of staff for comment.

"I agree with Gordon, Madam President. It's making the best of the hand we've been dealt."

"Okay, both of you. With whom and when should we discuss this?"

Black looked to Gordon.

He nodded and addressed the President. "The fewer the better, because it will be leaked. The chief justice can be first. He won't let it out. I'd wait as long as possible before telling anyone in the Senate. They'll all want to be the ones to put their finger in the dike. Charles . . ." he said, asking for confirmation.

"I don't agree completely. We can't wait so long that it will be clear we were avoiding them. It's a tough call, but after all this is over, we've still got to live with the Senate. I would err a bit on risking a leak and getting to them early."

The President smiled, playing with the pearls in her necklace. "You two manage to get down to bedrock. You don't always agree, but you make my decision clear, if not easy." She looked at Gordon. "I've got to go along with Charles on this. We'll hold off as long as we can, but between a possible leak and waiting too long, I'll risk the press getting the story early."

He nodded, and gave Black a thumbs-up.

Julia Gold had been downtown in the police commissioner's office only once before, and that had been to attend a civic event. This time, she was there to plead for her position to charge Jacques Talleyrand as a co-conspirator in the death of Judd Arnold.

"How does this business about the justice not being a citizen change things?" the commissioner asked Chief Donovan.

"It provides motive."

"For whom to do what?"

"For the Roland woman to bang this reporter on the head if that's what he found."

"What about this man you said was hanging around?"

Chief Donovan summed up the case against Talleyrand. "By his own testimony, he was there either just before Arnold was killed or right after. The only evidence we have that he was there before the killing is circumstantial and indeterminate. He might very well have smothered the man himself, or talked Mrs. Roland into both of them doing it, but we can't prove either scenario. He's admitted that he helped to dispose of Arnold's body. Detective Gold believes this is a convenient cover, trading a lesser crime for first-degree murder, but the district attorney wants a case he can prove in court . . . and that ain't it."

Julia squirmed in her seat, but she kept quiet. "Speak only if the commissioner addresses you directly," Donovan had advised.

"Where does the DA stand with Talleyrand's plea?" the commissioner asked.

"They're still working on it," Donovan said. "The man's lawyers don't want him named in the same indictment as Mrs. Roland. I don't know why that's so damn important if he gets out on a plea anyway. The lawyer hired by Justice Chatrier to act on her mother's behalf is insisting they both get indicted for the killing and, after that, both (in effect) plead to *lessers*. Talleyrand is resisting that."

"But you admit the only case we have against Talleyrand is based on his admissions."

"Yes."

"Our job is done then," the commissioner said. He looked at Julia for the first time. "Let the legal eagles work it out," he said directly to her, then changed the subject. "Chief Donovan tells me, Detective, that you're doing a hell of a good job. Keep up the good work."

Thanks for nothing, flitted through Julia's mind as she shook hands and thanked the commissioner before she and Donovan made their exit.

"Charles," said Senator Minturn, "to what do I owe the pleasure of your call? I bet you've got some more good news for us."

"How'd you guess, Henry?"

"Oh, I don't know, just lucky. So, what is it this time?"

"Justice Chatrier was not born in the United States. She's not a citizen."

Following a pause and a short snort, he croaked, "She's not a citizen of the United States?"

"That's correct."

"Are you serious?"

"There's evidence she was born in Martinique and never naturalized," he said, waiting for Minturn's mental digestion to run its course.

"Charles, do you know what this means? You're telling me we put an illegal alien on the Supreme Court?"

"It looks that way, Senator." Charles Black counted to ten before Minturn rejoined the conversation.

"Thank God, this is not my election year. Why didn't the bureau pick this up in their SPIN?"

"Joan has a birth certificate, a passport, and was admitted to the D.C. Bar. They'd check all that, but unless there was something that didn't seem right, I don't think they'd look behind it."

"So who did . . . as you say . . . look behind it?"

"A writer who's been researching an article on the justice. He found an airline passenger list or something, showing that she'd had her daughter with her when she arrived, and that the child's name was changed later from Jeanine to Joan for a birth certificate issued in New Orleans."

"So this is all coming out?"

"Without a doubt."

"No way of keeping it quiet?"

"No."

"When will she announce her resignation? She's got to do it with a big mea culpa."

"We don't think that's the way to go."

Minturn paused, and when he came back he did it with a snort that sounded like a wounded grizzly bear. "Why does that not surprise me? What's your boss' plan this time?"

"It's more like my plan."

"Are you going to let me in on it?"

Black looked at his notes. "The President makes her a citizen the moment it breaks, and we issue a press release, pointing out that Joan's confirmation was a near unanimous vote, that she'll make a great justice, and that none of this was her doing. Her mother did something stupid a long time ago that Joan knew nothing about."

"But if she was confirmed to the court as a non-citizen, she has no right to be there."

"Technically, not correct. The Constitution does not specify that justices of the Supreme Court need be citizens."

Black thought it was typical of Minturn not to admit what he didn't know. "No one would ever be confirmed who wasn't," he said.

"You mean before now."

"If we'd known."

"But Joan didn't know, either."

"Who's going to believe that?"

"It's true enough, and she did have a birth certificate."

"Charles, I need to think about this. Your point is, I guess, that letting her take the fall means we all go down with her. So we bare our souls to the American people . . . most of whom, I have to admit, did like her on television . . . and make her a citizen. Will the chief justice go along with it?"

"She's talking with him as we speak."

"Why didn't that lawyer, Cox, see this coming?" Henry snorted. "I knew we'd regret this choice."

It was time for Black to move on. Recriminations were not his passion. "Okay, Henry, I'll be in touch."

SPIN IT

Bryon Colder's article, when it came out simultaneously with a short version in the *Washington Post* and with a longer piece in Bernard's national magazine, caused a mixed reaction in the Arnold household.

"Did you call Chicago?" Adelaide Arnold asked her husband.

"They aren't sure at this point that it was premeditated murder, but they have evidence on who killed him. They won't tell me anymore."

"Are they idiots?"

"Now, Ad, don't get all worked up here."

"Someone . . . we're not being told who . . . in that house killed our son, and you tell me not to get worked up?"

"It's not going to bring him back, Ad. We'll find out the real story soon enough."

"I'm calling our congressman. I want this business investigated."

Arnold threw up his hands. "Okay, he doesn't like our President much. Maybe you'll get some action there."

"Damn right, I'll get some action. I'm calling the *Times,* too. What are they doing about it?"

"Judd wasn't out there on assignment, Ad."

"How do you know?"

"You mean they're lying to us?"

"He worked for the IHT. They're not bashful about boasting that Judd found out the new justice isn't a citizen. They should also be screaming on the front page about this, but there's hardly a word."

"Okay, Ad, I'll call the paper."

Kate received calls from both her mother and her father.

"Looks like he screwed it up this time," her mother said.

She took a deep breath. "Yes, Mother, but it's wonderful when the man you love really needs you."

"Don't be so damn cute, Daughter. It's not becoming."

She scolded herself for falling into the trap her mother had set. "What did you read or hear, Mother?"

She heard the pleasure in her mother's voice as she spoke. "The *Times* and the *Washington Post*. The President, with help from your magic man, put an illegal on the Supreme Court. History's going to have fun with that one."

"I guess you're right, but I have to tell you, Mother, life in Washington is not boring."

"So, how's she taking it?"

"She?"

"The President, Silly. She's got to be blaming your boyfriend."

She knew "Silly" was her mother's synonym for stupid. She tried to make it funny that her mother could never bring herself to mention Gordon by name, but it seldom worked. "Maybe she is," she said, "but I think everyone is trying to figure out how it got by the FBI."

"The boy who was killed . . . didn't you know him?"

"I'm sorry, Mother, but I'm not going there."

"Why not, for goodness sakes? He was . . . ."

She clicked the red button on her Blackberry . . . *lost connection. Damn that AT&T.*

Robert Stevens called from LA at his usual late night hour. Unlike her mother, Father called her at home, speaking with Gordon if she wasn't there.

"Hi, Kitten, looks like you guys have tied into a hummer."

"It's created a lot of noise, Father, but no panic here."

"Is she really not a citizen?"

"I don't know anymore than you do," she said.

"But how can that happen? God, the President must be having a stroke."

"She always asks about you, Father. Why don't you give her a call?"

Stevens paused. He understood this was Kate's way of getting him off the subject. He made it fun. "Maybe I will. Who escorts her around to all the social things she attends?"

"She could use a handsome man on her arm, Father."

"How old do you think she is?"

"Sixty."

"She doesn't look it. Are you sure?"

"How old are you?"

"You know damn well how old I am."

"Fifty?"

"Right, so she's too old for me."

"And she probably wouldn't move to California."

"I wouldn't blame her. They might kill her if she came out here."

"Father!"

"Sorry, but that scuttles it. So, what's going on in your sweet life?"

"I'm not a law clerk any longer."

"Does that make you happy?"

"I guess so."

"Good. What's next? Why can't you come out here for a week? I miss your cheery smile."

"I'll see what we can do, Father dear."

"No maybes, just do it."

"I'll work it out."

"That's my girl."

Kate smiled. She missed not seeing her father as often as she'd like. "Bye, Father . . . love you."

"Love you, too, Kitten. Say hello to Gordon for me."

The White House issued a brief statement, following a synopsis of Colder's article in the *Washington Post*:

"The President stands behind the selection of Joan Chatrier as a worthy member of the Supreme Court bench, confirmed by an almost unanimous vote in the United States Senate. The President hopes she will stay on the court and serve out her term. She is an innocent victim in a series of events that should never have happened."

"Who wrote that piece?" Kate asked Gordon as they put their feet up in the den and shared a wedge of soft cheese with a glass of wine.

"It's an art form. Take a volatile situation, use nice words, and say nothing."

"Is that a recent invention?" she asked, tongue in cheek.

"I doubt it."

"I don't think the President's plain-talking role model, Harry Truman, used it."

"Maybe, but then he never went to college," Gordon said, adding a smile and a wink, but he could see Kate had more on her mind. "What's going through that nimble brain of yours?" he asked.

She was serious. "What if this is not over?"

Gordon nodded. "You're right. Joan needs to prove herself on the court for the President and all the rest of us to come out of the situation in good shape."

"No, I mean what if you're all on the wrong track?"

Gordon had been paying more attention to putting cheese on the crackers than to what Kate was saying. "You mean like Joan is really a KGB agent?"

She disliked not being taken seriously, but she smiled. "Judd Arnold did not need to go to Chicago to confront Mari Roland on the issue of

Joan's citizenship. If that was all he found, he had all the evidence he needed in his hot little hand . . . not so little, actually."

Gordon was still paying less than 100% attention. "So why did he go?"

"What if there was something else?"

"Like what?"

Why doesn't he listen? "I don't know," she said, annoyance in her voice, "but I don't think it had anything to do with Philippe Talleyrand either. Please consider that you guys may be making a mistake not letting Joan resign."

"What do you know that we don't?"

"I doubt she's with the KGB," she said, "and when I figure it out, you'll be the first to know. But if I were the President, I'd let her resign."

The mood in Congress shifted from questioning the President to criticism of all concerned. Many Senators acted as if they'd been personally affronted. None took any responsibility for confirming what they now considered a bad choice by the President. The next stop on that voyage would be outspoken opposition to Joan remaining on the court. Charles Black needed to regain some initiative.

Gordon called Joan Chatrier at Black's suggestion. The White House needed help in getting the press and Congress off their back.

"Joan, the press is going to hound you to death. The gloves are off in Congress. Several members of the opposition party in the House have scheduled a special hearing, and they're kicking it off with a press conference. They're going to accuse the White House of a cover-up. We need to get the country on the President's side in this. You're the one to do it."

"Gordon, I don't know. Maybe I should resign and get it over with. I'm a trial lawyer. That's what I ought to be doing. This controversy has done one good thing. It's recharged my batteries. Now, all I need is a few good clients."

"It's your call, Joan, but you've still got the citizenship issue to deal with. If we do it her way, the President can make you a citizen by decree and moot the issue without your admitting anything."

"I appreciate that. What's the position of the chief justice? Last time he and I spoke, he was supportive. He's certainly spoken to the President in the interim."

"He's not objecting to this course of action. He's not easy to read, but I think he likes having you alongside. He wants to talk with you, however, before you meet with the press."

"All right, then. Let's get it over with."

Kate called Gordon when she heard about the press conference. "I hope you know what you're doing, Gordon. Why don't you let her resign before the other shoe can drop?"

He knew what she thought, and while he didn't agree with her, he no longer took her position lightly. "She's an innocent in all this, Kate. I don't think the President has any choice but to stick with her."

Kate was adamant. "*Innocent* is an interesting . . . and relative . . . term, Gordon. The President could say how sorry she is that this happened, but she understands why the jurist feels resignation is the best thing for all."

"Is this what you really think?"

"Yes, something's rotten in Denmark, and, as they say, it's not just the cheese."

"We have no evidence that Judd Arnold found anything."

"I know you think I have it in for Joan Chatrier, but I really don't. Judd did not go out to Chicago to tell Mari Roland he'd found that Joan was not a citizen. He must have discovered something else. I knew the guy. I know the way he'd think."

"Kate, I hope to hell you're wrong. The President wants Joan to stay on the court, and that's the end of it. In the meantime, may I ask you to attend her press conference? I can't be there."

"A labor of love for my baby."

"Thanks."

"Will you be in the office?"

"Yup. I'll tell Emily to put you right through to me, regardless."

"I thought that was a standing order," Kate said, laughing. "Don't worry. I'll call you as soon as it's over."

The pressroom was filled to the rafters with T.V. cameras, reporters, and interested persons with enough influence or the good luck to obtain a pass. Joan Chatrier gave a five-minute introductory talk, summarizing the occasion of her mother's entry into the country and her own early life in New Orleans. She purposefully did not embroider the story with her long line of successes from high school on. Then, the questions started coming.

Kate could see, watching Joan as she stood before the television cameras, that she was becoming more and more stressed as the session progressed. Reporters repeated their questions with minor changes and in a manner, if not designed to annoy, certainly had that effect, making it seem to Joan that no one trusted her. She tightened up, and her answers became quick and monosyllabic. Near the end of the session, the questioning took an unforeseen turn.

"Justice Chatrier, Josh Abrams of Associated Media. Can you describe your reaction when you were told you had a brother, and how did that change or intensify when you heard he might be learning disabled?"

"Yes, that was . . ." She stopped to reach into her pocket for a tissue. "Excuse me a moment," she said, and you could hear a pin drop in the pressroom before she continued.

"Well, yes, that was a shock. I won't deny it. At first, I was a little angry . . . strike that . . . upset," she said with the beginning of a smile and twinkle in her eye following light responsive laughter in the room, "at my mother for not telling me. Later . . . I mean, moments later . . . I was happy, amazingly happy, to learn that I might have a brother. Yes, I was told he might not be an Einstein, but that wouldn't matter to me. I haven't met him yet, but I'm looking forward to it very much."

The same reporter raised his hand. "A follow up, please, if I may."

Joan nodded.

"How did it make you feel, Justice Chatrier, when you heard your mother was named by the district attorney in Chicago as the person who killed the *Herald Tribune* reporter, Judd Arnold? Second degree murder, I believe is the charge he said he was preparing to send to the Grand Jury."

Joan did a double take. "I don't think that charge has actually been made . . . " she said, at which point she was drowned out by a clamor in the back of the room. Several reporters spoke in unison.

"Yes, she was named . . . this morning. It came over the wires."

Joan seemed stunned by the news. After a moment she thrust her head back and slammed her fist on the lectern, knocking over three microphones. "Well, I'll tell you what. You all can be the first to know. We're not going to let this stand. My mother's going to have another damn good lawyer in her corner . . . me . . . and now, this press conference is over."

On her way out, several of the reporters shot questions at her.

"Your mother's dead, why are you . . . "

"She didn't murder anyone," Joan shot back. "We'll set that straight."

BACK OFFICE POLITICS

Kate got Gordon out of a meeting in his own conference room. "Gordon, it looks like she's quitting the court."

"What?"

"The DA in Chicago has named her mother as Judd's killer. When Joan was told, she lost it. She slammed her fist on the podium, and said she would defend her mother's reputation. She also said her mother was going to have another good lawyer in her corner . . . 'me' . . . and then she walked out. It'll be all over the news."

"How long ago?"

"Minutes. I just came out of the room. Everybody here is calling someone. The T.V. cameras have it all on tape."

"Thanks for being Katie on the spot, Beautiful. I'd better get over to the White House."

While Gordon spoke with Kate, his assistant, Emily, took a call from Charles Black.

"The chief's in the Oval Office, Mr. Cox. He asked that you join them as soon as possible."

"I'm on my way."

Gordon arrived as a news broadcast of Joan Chatrier's press conference was being replayed.

"That's powerful stuff, Madam President," Charles Black said as Gordon appeared in the doorway of the Oval Office in the company of the President's secretary.

"Hello, Gordon," the President said. "I think you know everyone here."

Gordon nodded a greeting to the chief justice of the Supreme Court, Senator Henry Minturn, the attorney general, and he smiled at Charles Black as he took the open seat next to him.

"That was a surprise," the President said. "You didn't see it coming, did you, Gordon?"

"No, I sure didn't, Madam President," he said, "but are we certain she resigned?"

Black answered. "It was an emotional and sudden response, I guess, to the pressures and events of recent months. They caught up with her, and she lashed out. I don't think it was something she planned. Perhaps, but it looked completely spontaneous to me, and you may be right, Gordon, I don't think she used the word resign."

"Play it again, Sam," the President said to the young man running the CD player.

They all watched, Gordon for the first time.

The President allowed him a moment to assemble his thoughts. "Do you agree with Charles, Gordon?"

He focused on the President. "Joan didn't plan that, and I didn't hear a resignation."

"So what do we do now, gentlemen?" the President asked.

Minturn was the first to respond. "Let her resign. You've made your case, Madam President. It was an honest mistake by all of us, and that's been pretty well accepted. Let's end it, for Christ's sake."

"Nothing's changed, Henry," the President said. "Yesterday, she was still our choice for the court. If we walk away now, it will look like there's more to it, and the press will never give it or me a moment's rest." She looked to Gordon for support.

He nodded. "I would sit tight, Madam President," he said. "If Joan resigns, you can express regret. If she doesn't, let her time on the court speak for itself. This story will get old quickly." As he said the last few words, Kate's earlier warning came through to him loud and clear: "What if it was something else that Judd Arnold found?" But he said nothing.

No consensus was reached among those present, but Gordon and Black came close to one. The chief justice spoke only when the President asked him a question, but Gordon could see he hoped Joan would tender her resignation. Maybe the chief justice and Kate were right . . . let her resign and get on with it. The attorney general spoke in and out of turn and, in Gordon's opinion, too long and too often. Charles Black, using Gordon's logic, summed it up.

"Madam President, this event can be a blessing in disguise. Joan Chatrier, in a very real sense that most Americans can and will understand, is a heroine. At the press conference she promised to defend her mother's reputation. The aspects of this case involving her citizenship, or lack thereof, are lost in the emotions of the moment. You can grant her citizenship just to be certain, not to help an illegal alien or even admit she is or isn't a citizen, but to remove any impediment to letting her mother rest in peace. I would do it, and I'd do it right away while you still have a free pass. If Joan Chatrier's mother killed this young man, it's a tragedy, but it has nothing to do with her daughter's remaining on the court. We've got to move fast, before she really does resign. As Henry said, they're already raising hell up and down the aisles in Congress."

The President looked around the room. Henry Minturn snorted, but nodded his agreement. The chief justice retained his poker face. The AG started to say something, but fell silent when the President's eyes shifted quickly to Gordon, who quietly nodded that he also agreed with Charles Black's conclusion.

"All right, gentlemen," the President said with a sly smile, "any suggestions on who we send to talk Joan into staying on the court?"

All eyes turned to Gordon Cox.

Kate, at Gordon's suggestion, put a call in to Julia Gold to see if anything had changed.

"I'm under strict orders not to discuss any aspect of the Arnold killing with anyone. It came down from the top, Kate. I'm sorry. The case and the pleadings will go before a special Grand Jury in three days. Until that's run its course, we're all under a tight wrap here. You can call the DA's office, but I know they won't comment. The DA's been under a lot of political pressure here, led by that woman from New York who's still shouting about a conspiracy."

"I understand."

"Ever get to Chicago?"

"Sure. I'll call you, and you do the same. Come on down and we'll give you the ten cent tour."

"I may do that someday."

"You're welcome any time, Julia," and Kate made the offer sound like it was coming from a friend.

It took twenty-four hours, but Joan Chatrier finally returned the call Gordon left on her answering service.

"It's a mess, Gordon."

"I have a small bit of good news for you. The President made you a citizen, effective yesterday. They've arranged for the chief justice to swear you in."

"That's nice, but I'm not destroying my birth certificate, just so you know."

"Have you tried to get in touch with Talleyrand?"

"Not yet. I've been subpoenaed to appear in court in Chicago in two weeks. I understand Jacques Talleyrand will be there. Maybe we'll meet then."

"I wouldn't count on it."

Chatrier laughed. "I guess you've got that right, Gordon, but sooner or later he'll have to meet with me."

Gordon liked hearing Joan laugh again. There was hope. "What's your plan?" he asked.

"Well, first I need to speak with the chief justice."

"I just met with him and the President. They want you to stay on the court."

There was a long silence before Joan responded. "Can I really do that, Gordon?"

He was ready. "What's changed from a few days ago?"

"Mother might be indicted posthumously."

"Maybe, maybe not. It hasn't happened yet. I don't think the Grand Jury's in session. Anyway, it's nothing you did."

"I don't know, Gordon. Scandals have wide perimeters."

He pressed on, bargaining for more time to let her make a reasoned decision. "At least give it a few days, and let the White House issue a press release supporting you 100%. We'll see what happens. Frankly, the President thinks you'll carry any national poll by at least 60/40 in spite of the opposition in Congress. That opposition is all political name-calling aimed mostly at the White House."

"So I wait for the Congress to try to impeach me?"

"On what grounds?"

"I don't know . . . that I'm clearly not a nice person?"

A joke . . . we're getting through it, he thought. "You'll make a great Supreme Court justice."

"Okay, Gordon, if you say the chief justice wants me to stay, but I'm going to spend a week on the beach. If that's a problem for anyone, then all bets are off."

"Where?"

"Martinique, where else?"

"Let me know if I can do anything to help."

"I'll do that."

"And don't change your mind."

He wasn't sure, but he thought Joan said, "Drop dead," as she put down the phone.

Emily buzzed her boss. "Charles Black is coming over. He said it would only take a few minutes. It sounded important."

"So wrap it up for me, Gordon," Charles said as he settled into a chair in Gordon's office and Emily closed the door. "Where do we stand on our favorite Supreme Court justice?"

Gordon knew the President was taking a beating in the press. He was aware that members of Congress on the President's side of the aisle blamed him. He concentrated now on looking at the case against Joan's mother through Charles' eyes.

"In Joan's opinion, the Chicago DA's taking the easy way out for himself and giving a pass to Talleyrand. Joan intends to make them both prove their case. She needs to have access to all the police records, and the only way to do that is to defend her mother. She hired a good Illinois criminal defense attorney to act on her mother's behalf. Here's a copy of the letter Joan received from her mother's lawyer. It's very interesting."

Black took the letter from him and read it.

> *Dear Madam Justice,*
>
> *The Illinois court in Chicago held a one judge hearing to determine if there was need for a full blown jury trial to determine the deceased Mari Roland's guilt or innocence of second degree murder, and to act on my motion for access to the full police record supporting the indictment. The judge found the prosecution's case depended completely upon the sworn testimony of Jacques Talleyrand, who swears that he saw Judd Arnold's dead body on the floor at Mrs. Roland's feet, that she had the weapon in her hand, and that the two of them acted to cover it up. There is no corroborating evidence of Talleyrand's being in Chicago besides an airline ticket; no fingerprints; and he was not given the opportunity to be picked out of a line-up. At this point,*

I'm not sure holding a trial before a jury is avoidable to exonerate your mother, unless, of course, Talleyrand were to recant his confession. We have not been able to convince the DA to have the indictment, if any, issued in both their names, followed by two pleas.

Talleyrand's confession to being an accomplice is apparently sufficient for the District Attorney, but his case to prove Mrs. Roland's guilt beyond a reasonable doubt has some pretty big holes in it. Prosecution records were ordered turned over to me. Meanwhile, formal sentencing of Jacques Talleyrand for his plea-bargained admission to being an accessory is pending outcome of the criminal trial. Any ideas, Madam Justice? Let me know how you wish to proceed.

Charles placed the paper back on his desk without comment. "I'm meeting with Henry Minturn tomorrow morning, Gordon. What's the best/worst scenario?"

Gordon understood what the President's chief of staff was asking him. "It depends on how the DA in Chicago decides to handle the case. If it goes to trial, Joan Chatrier is going to be front page for quite a while. If they drop it, we might have a political problem in the Senate, but the press has bigger fish to fry."

"What do we know about this DA?"

"This is Chicago, remember. Kate made a call to the detective who handled the case, but the lid is on out there. I would say the answer is in that letter," he said, pointing at the page Black had just read. "I don't think the DA is going to try a case against the mother of a Supreme Court justice if he doesn't think he can win it hands down."

"You think it will end there?"

"If Joan lets it."

"You mean, if she doesn't insist on some kind of formal clearance for her mother?"

"Exactly." Saving his conscience by meeting Kate halfway, he said, "Maybe Joan needs to make a decision. Either stay on the court or start chasing windmills, but not both."

"Can you speak with her, Gordon?"

"Sure, but I think she's finished listening to me."

"Should the President write her a note?"

"And have that leaked to the press . . . absolutely not. The White House stays as far away from this as possible."

"She'll be asked about it at the next press conference."

"She should refuse to comment until we know for sure what Joan's going to do," Gordon said.

"How long before we know?"

"Joan doesn't have much time, and she knows it."

Charles Black nodded, picked up the letter from the edge of Gordon's desk, and glanced through it again. "I see what you mean about the case against Joan's mother. Sounds like her lawyer has a plea bargain up his sleeve."

"That's right, Charles, very perceptive."

Black rose from his chair. "Okay, I've enough to keep Henry in fighting trim for a few days. Thanks, Gordon. Let me know when you hear from Justice Chatrier."

THE FRENCH CONNECTION

Kate had often used her long walk home from Capitol Hill as a time to free up her mind and shake off the trials of the day. On these occasions, stoplights and reckless drivers could distract her, but she was otherwise oblivious to her surroundings. She was in the same mood returning from a workout, jogging around the Lagoon.

In all that had gone on with Joan Chatrier's nomination and confirmation, little attention had been paid to the tragedy that was Judd Arnold. Kate needed closure, and no one was providing it for her. What had he found? She'd always had difficulty accepting the popular notion that it was Joan's citizenship, or lack thereof. She knew Byron Colder had dug that up, but official records speak for themselves, don't they? Why would Judd have gone to Chicago to gain confirmation on that issue?

If Judd had found something else, where had he made the discovery? If in New Orleans, Colder should have seen it too. Had he brought it from Paris? She doubted he'd ever thought about Joan before he arrived in Louisiana. She thought back on her discussions in the *Times* D.C. office with the chatty Mary Watts. And Kate knew now it had been Judd who'd called her that night as she and Gordon had arrived home. Had he needed advice? What a difference a few seconds could make. She always met the same brick wall. Judd hadn't let anyone, except perhaps Mari Roland, in on his secret. She fought to hold back the tears.

More and more Kate thought the answer lay with Mari Roland, maybe something from her past. Everyone had been concentrating on Joan's life, but what about Mari? Kate had always wondered why Mari lived on the Southside of Chicago, at the same time calling every day to check on her daughter. From what had Mari Roland been hiding? Kate knew Judd Arnold. He would not have gone to Chicago just to rub it in.

Gordon was talking on the phone when she arrived home. He greeted her with one hand over the speaker, "Only be a moment."

She threw him a kiss before disappearing into their bedroom to change and shower.

Gordon was off the phone when she reappeared. "I have some news, Kate, but you probably won't like to hear it."

She moved quickly in his direction, plopped down on his lap, put her arms around his neck, and gave him a silencing kiss. He picked her up and carried her to the couch, where he sat down with her still on his lap.

"So what is it, Big Boy?" she said, laughing.

"That was Charles Black on the phone. Chatrier came back from her week in the French part of the Caribbean recharged and fully committed to serving out her term on the court."

A light went on in her brain. "That's it," she said, turning in Gordon's lap to face him, eyes wide open and almost throttling him.

"What is what?" he coughed.

"The French connection . . . New Orleans, but also Martinique." *She should have seen it before. It opened the door through the brick wall she'd been running up against.* "Don't you remember us sitting right here that Sunday we came back from New York? You were telling me something about the Department of Justice research on Joan's life turning up something about Martinique."

"That's where her mother was born. Is that what you mean?"

"Yes, but it was something more," she said.

Gordon moved his jaw around. "I remember the DOJ had some concern about Joan having gone to Cuba. All that came up at the hearing, too, but it turned out to be nothing."

She shook her finger to get her mind working. "Now I remember. We talked about there being some connection between Cuba and Martinique. What was the name of that young lawyer assigned to us when we were in Havana?"

Gordon shook his head. "The French have a love affair with revolution," he said, with a twinkle in his eye. "There was sympathy in France for the Cuban revolution during the time before Castro came out of the closet as a communist bully."

She grabbed Gordon by both shoulders and shook him. "When? When did that take place?"

"1958."

Kate paused for full effect . . . "The year before Mari came to New Orleans."

"What's your 'what if'?"

That brought a big smile. "What if . . . it wasn't Joan who had the contact with Cuba? What if . . . it was Mari?"

Julia Gold sat with her chief and a lawyer from the district attorney's office behind closed doors. The lawyer was talking.

"The news about Joan Chatrier not being a citizen hasn't changed the determination of Mari Roland's defense. We've been put on notice by the Roland's defense counsel that he'll go the whole way toward making us prove our case beyond a reasonable doubt. You people have also heard, no doubt, that her daughter, the Supreme Court justice, is going to force the issue."

"Attorney Wilson's bluffing," the chief said.

"I don't think so, and with all the press on the case so far, we're going to get more than the usual coverage for any trial. The DA's afraid we'll all come out looking pretty bad."

"You mean, he'll look bad," Julia mumbled to herself.

When the state's lawyer had left them alone, Donovan gave Julia her orders. "I know you don't think this is what happened. But maybe it will help your analysis by proving the negative. I want to put this damn case to bed, and it won't die."

"That's because we haven't figured it out yet."

"Okay, Gold, step by step, your assignment is to review all of the evidence and give the DA the case against Mari Roland based upon hard facts . . . only hard facts . . . without Talleyrand's testimony."

The DA wasn't impressed. "I'll tell you again . . . I hope for the last time . . . I'm not taking that factual picture to court. No jury I've ever been in front of would buy it. All the equities are in the other direction. On the other hand, we have Talleyrand's admission against interest that will make the jury sit up and take notice if we charge Mari Roland."

"Is it an 'admission against interest' when the only other person with knowledge is dead?" Julia asked.

He nodded that she had a point. "I believe Talleyrand will be persuasive, but I'll tell you the truth," the DA said, "I don't really want to try that case, either."

In Georgetown, Joan Chatrier, burdened by the news from her mother's lawyer that the Chicago district attorney had refused to include Talleyrand in the same charge with Mari, decided to accept Jacques Talleyrand's invitation to meet personally with him and discuss her case brought against him to have her old passport declared valid.

She'd had her complaint in the passport case typed up, signed, and served on Talleyrand, but they'd held off filing it in the Federal District Court. This was a tactic that had often worked for her in reaching an early settlement to trials she handled on behalf of others. She wanted her charges to bring out Jacque's role in falsifying her birth certificate, and he would have little choice but to vigorously defend himself if she filed the complaint. Doing it this way, she strategized, gave her some leverage that she hoped to use in defending her mother's reputation before the Illinois State Court in Chicago. She'd also take the opportunity while there to meet her alleged half brother, Philippe.

These meetings required Joan to visit the house that had been her home during her time in New Orleans. Doubts about this decision began to filter in on the limo ride to Reagan National. By the time she arrived in New Orleans, doubts had grown into serious apprehension. There was nothing rational about her uneasiness. Her entire life had been composed of taking on one unseen enemy after another. Why had this meeting with Jacques Talleyrand suddenly thrown such foreboding into her heart?

The meeting with Philippe Talleyrand loomed large in front of her as she and her Protective Services officer approached the Talleyrand home in a limousine rented at the airport.

"How much of this," Jacques Talleyrand asked, sweeping his arms to encompass their surroundings, "do you remember, Madam Justice?" as the two of them settled into the same sitting room off the library where the man had met earlier with Detective Julia Gold.

"Very little," she said.

"You were quite young, and you didn't know many English words."

Joan took a steadying breath.

Her host took her coolness in stride. "Philippe is waiting to see you. We can do that now or later. Your choice."

This took Joan by surprise. Meeting Philippe had been a condition on which she'd insisted, but she'd expected to meet resistance when the moment arrived. "Later is all right," she said. Then, with the same tone she might have used to address a recalcitrant witness before her in court, she demanded, "Let's talk about what really happened in Chicago."

Talleyrand showed no sign of being intimidated. "What part of what I told the Chicago police don't you understand?"

Joan looked piercingly at him, but when she spoke her voice was filled with emotion, not the cool detachment of a trial lawyer confronting an adversary. "I understand what you told them. I just don't believe it."

Talleyrand's eyebrows curled upward. He rose from his chair, knocked it away with his hip, and slammed both hands down on the desk in front of him. The larger than life presence he projected changed the balance between them. Joan sat frozen in her chair as he bored in on her.

"What don't you believe? That your mother, in a moment of panic, could not have struck out at this man, who was leaving her home to tell the world something about you? Is that what you don't understand?"

A few seconds passed without Joan being aware.

Jacques Talleyrand stood firm, but his voice became more conciliatory. "I never thought for a moment that she intended to kill him. When I came in the door she was standing there, whispering over and again that she hadn't meant to hit him so hard."

"I know she would have told me," Joan said in a voice close to a whisper.

"Exactly when would she have done that?" he asked, resuming an aggressive stance.

"The night before she died . . . when we spoke on the phone. She would have told me then."

"And what would you have done?" Talleyrand demanded.

"We'd have worked it out in a plea."

"And have the truth paraded around the world that your mother had murdered a journalist?"

Joan hesitated. "If it came to that, yes."

He took precise aim. Joan stared up at herself in a man's clothes, a barrister going in for the kill. "What do you mean, 'if'?" he said, mocking her. "And you would put your own life and career aside in order to defend your mother?"

"Yes, of course."

"And what would she have thought about that . . . you putting her welfare ahead of your own?"

"She always did the right thing in the end."

"Exactly, but what in her mind would have been the right thing, Joan? Maybe that's exactly what she did do."

"I could have talked her out of killing herself."

"Sure, if she gave you the chance, but she didn't . . . did she?" And with that Jacques seemed to rest his case.

Joan felt close to tears as Jacques moved to end it with a more understanding turn of phrase, carefully enunciating each word. "You know, as I do, that there's nothing your mother would not have done to assure your success. I don't think she meant to kill that young man, but she was perfectly capable of striking out at anyone who had you in their sights." Then, as if some inspiration came to him, he said, "Let me ask you this . . . did she ever tell you anything about your father?"

Joan, trying without success to hold back tears, could only shake her head.

"I didn't think so," he said.

"Why not?" She barely got out the words.

"Because it was better for you not to know. If it were something that would help you, then she'd have told you."

"Maybe she didn't know."

"Why do you think she lived buried in the bowels of Chicago?"

Joan's heart skipped a beat as she waited for the next shoe to drop.

Talleyrand blinked, shaking his head in disbelief. "Do you really believe she didn't know who your father was?" he asked.

The subject of her father, Joan was forced to admit, was not one that she'd felt she needed to pursue since her teenage years. "She wouldn't have killed herself for that," she said.

"That might depend on who he is."

"Do you know?" Joan asked.

"No," he said, sitting back down in his chair. "But if I did, I probably wouldn't tell you either." He paused again, seeming to consider whether he should say what was on his mind. "I never had any doubt from the first time I met Mari that she knew damn well who had fathered her daughter."

Joan wiped away her tears.

Talleyrand was quiet, until she looked up at him. "There's another thing you should understand. I was very much in love with your mother. I asked her to marry me before Philippe was born. It took me a long time to get over her not being here to share this big house. I was proud to have influence sufficient to obtain a birth certificate for you. I honestly believe I would do that again tomorrow, if she were here and asked me. I begged her to come back with me that day in Chicago. Do you know what she said?"

Joan frowned.

"She said that you wouldn't understand."

"I still don't," Joan said . . . gathering force in her voice.

Talleyrand stood erect, taking her comment as more of an insult than Joan might have intended.

"Okay, have it your way, but what happened, happened, and I don't think the way it all ended up for you is . . . well things could have been worse for you . . . much worse."

Joan remained silent.

Jacques moved around from behind his desk. "Would you like to go now and meet your mother's other child?" he said. "He was injured while in her womb, but he's a loveable person."

She wiped more tears from her eye, nodded, and slowly rose to her feet. After informing her Protection Services officer what she was doing, she followed several paces behind Talleyrand to an elevator that took them to the second floor. The long hallways, with high ceilings all dimly lighted, seemed foreign at her current eye level. At first nothing seemed familiar, but as they came closer to the wing that Philippe now called home, she began to move back in time. She remembered traveling along these same jagged routes at a much lower level, skipping and laughing from the bedrooms at the end of the hall, down the back stairs to the large kitchen and the lighted fireplace in the maid's sitting room, where she loved to lie on the big sofa and play with her dolls. It was all coming back in three-dimensional black and white. The bright, energetic young girl she saw in these glimpses of her past shocked her. There were no colors in her memory bank, but the scene recalled a surprisingly happy childhood with love in every corner.

She looked for memories of her mother, but no specifics came through the haze, only a remarkable sense of . . . *this is it, I'm finally where I belong.*

What had changed young Mari's world? Had it been the conception of Philippe? Or the reality brought on as it would appear to an African American woman from Martinique living in a grand house in New Orleans in the 1960s? Was that why she'd taken her daughter and run?

A HEAVENLY REUNION

Joan Chatrier arrived at her half brother's quarters composed and comfortable with her surroundings. The walk around the home had given her a sense of who she was that had been missing for all the years in between. She felt alert and strangely at peace with herself. She would draw on that strength in the minutes that lay ahead.

Philippe Talleyrand was shorter than Joan expected. She guessed that was due to the injury Mari had sustained during her pregnancy. His shoulders were as broad as Jacques' but seemed much closer to the rest of his body. He sat at a young person's table in a small chair that squeezed his hips. His father noticed Joan's reaction.

"He was given that desk set as a child. He sits there for hours, writing and talking to his imaginary friends."

She smiled at her brother, and moved closer. "How are you today, my friend?"

"Who wants to know?" Philippe asked, without looking up from the paper on which he was writing in sure strokes, not scribbling. His complexion was sandy colored and his skin smooth. With no facial hair, he projected a very handsome, boyish image if you took him at face value.

"What's that you're working on?" Joan asked in a tone of voice void of condescension. She was truly interested in his work.

"What's it to you?" a boy's voice said clearly, as if for the record, still not looking up from his work.

"Well, it must be very important. You write so beautifully."

Philippe raised his head and saw her for the first time. She noticed the slightest twitch of a smile.

"I write good," he said.

"I can see that. What's your name?"

It sounded like "Fleep" when he pronounced it.

"That's a smart name, Philippe. What's your last name?"

The boy in half a man's body glanced at Jacques Talleyrand. "Like his," he said, smiling and pointing.

At least you know who your father is, she thought. She looked at Jacques Talleyrand, shifting her position so she could see both men without turning her head. "Where's your mother?"

Philippe followed her movements and seemed to light up. "She's in heaven now. She's very pretty. Would you like to see her picture?"

"Yes, I would, Philippe."

Philippe arose with some difficulty from the chair that stuck with him and fell unattended from his hips as he shuffled to the other side of the room. She remained where she was, watching as he returned with a framed photograph held in both hands.

"Here she is," he said, holding it out for her to see.

She focused on a color image of Mari Roland dancing for the camera when not more than twenty-two or -three years old. Mari wore a light summer dress, which twirled with her graceful movement and clung to her in all the right places. Her face was radiant and her smile a brilliant white surrounded by smooth ebony. Her mother's vitality and beauty took Joan's breath away.

"Oh, my goodness, your mother certainly is beautiful, Philippe."

"She's in Heaven now."

She fought to maintain her composure as the image of a small boy dressed in his father's shoes walked over and replaced the picture on the bookshelf.

"How old are you, Philippe?" she asked him.

"Old enough to know better," he said as he picked up his chair and sat down again at the desk.

"That's a good age to be." She laughed.

As if her laughter was contagious, Philippe looked up and laughed with her. When he did, she saw in him their mother's spirit.

Joan took a deep breath, still trying to hold back the tears, and decided she had to end it. "Well, I need to go now, Philippe. I live in Washington, D.C. Is there anything I can get for you up there?"

The 50-year-old boy thought for a moment. Still looking up at her from his seat, he spoke in a clear voice. "I need a white horse. Do you have any of those?"

"Oh, my, where would you keep it?" she asked, surprised by his request. She glanced at Jacques, who smiled and appeared proud of his son's performance.

"I have a big bed," Philippe said. "He could stay with me, and then when it's dark at night, he'll carry me across the sky." Philippe made a big round arc with his arms, emphasizing the sweep of his nighttime ride.

"Well, I'll see what I can come up with, Philippe, but I haven't seen any white horses recently. I think they're pretty hard to find."

"That's okay, but it has to be white and have wings. You can't see brown or black ones when the sky is dark."

She looked at Jacques, tears now streaming down her cheeks. He nodded. They left Philippe back at work in his cramped chair, moving his pencil across the pad on his desk.

Joan called her mother's lawyer shortly after arriving back in Georgetown. The visit to Philippe and his father had done more than build a bridge to her past. It brought her mother back to her. The tongue-lashing Jacques Talleyrand had administered uncovered a reality she'd long since buried.

Any bitterness she might have had toward their conspiracy to make her a citizen evaporated into the love and care for her that had produced the phony birth certificate. Philippe, as damaged as he was, gave her the connection to family she'd never had. It was time to consolidate her gains and get on with the life her mother had made for her.

"Mark, can you make a deal with the district attorney to reduce mother's charge to negligent homicide and let it go at that?"

"Probably. They can't win any other case. What about Talleyrand?"

"What's the point? Let him alone, so long as my mother doesn't go down in the annals as a murderer."

"All right, Joan, I'll call over there right now."

KATE'S WHAT IF

The news of the Chicago case being bargained by Joan Chatrier was greeted with relief at the White House. No one other than Kate and the man's parents had any thoughts for Judd Arnold, and the Justice had come through the ordeal with no more than a few scratches, which would heal with time. It was back to business as usual on Capitol Hill.

Charles called Gordon to express his congratulations for calling the outcome correctly, and to ask one more time whether Gordon thought there were any residuals to worry about. Gordon told Black that sometimes it was better to be lucky than smart. He mentioned Kate's theory that there must be more to the Judd Arnold story.

"Are you kidding me, Gordon? What's she found now?"

"It's more like what no one else has found. Kate knew this guy Arnold. She does not think he would have gone out to Chicago to get confirmation from Mari Roland that Joan was not born in the United States. He wouldn't have needed that anymore than Byron Colder did. She believes he found something more, and she's determined to find out what it was."

"Can't you tell her to let it go?"

"I'm not going to do that, Charles, and even if I did, it wouldn't slow her down more than a half second."

"Do you think she's really onto something?"

"I don't know, Charles, but I had to mention it."

"I dearly wish you hadn't. I've got enough things to keep me up all night."

"Hang in there, Charles. If she does find anything, you'll be the first to know."

Kate helped Gordon pack for yet another trip to the West Coast.

"Why don't you come along this time, Kate? This is too good an opportunity to pass up. You can pay that visit you've been promising your old man, and we can go on up the coast to Monterey to relax for a few days after I'm done in court."

She laughed. "My *old man* is only ten years older than you are, Gordon."

"I know, but being around you has made me younger."

"I'll take that as a compliment," she said. "But you're lucky I don't bring Mother into the conversation."

"You're absolutely right about that." He smiled, and closed his suitcase.

She wrapped her arms around her man's neck. "What if I call Father and meet you in LA in a few days? The small in-chambers party for Joan Chatrier that was postponed until her status got sorted out is being held tomorrow, and I'm invited. Joan actually called me yesterday. She made me promise to be there."

"Okay, good," he said. "See you in a few days." They embraced, and held on for an extra second or two.

Alone in the apartment after seeing Gordon off in his taxi to BWI, Kate poured herself a glass of white wine and sat looking out over the Potomac River, thinking about Judd Arnold. She explored the epiphany she'd reached while sitting on Gordon's lap days earlier . . . that maybe it was Mari . . . not Joan . . . who held the key to what Judd had discovered.

If he'd wanted to bring a multi-generational picture back to his readers in France, Judd might have blended Mari Roland's life into the story. Mari began that life on the French island of Martinique. Who knew what Judd Arnold might have discovered when he dove into that end of the pool.

Hiding from something or someone provided the best rationale in Kate's mind for Mari's refusal, for over thirty-five years, to leave her virtual cave on the Southside of Chicago. From what or whom was she escaping? This could also explain, as forcefully as Joan's citizenship issue, why Mari had taken that secret to her grave.

Kate cast off her own more traditional approach to fact-finding, and focused on sources that would have been easily available to Judd, but a bit off the radar screen of others, such as Byron Colder. She thought about the articles Mary Watts told her Judd had copied from the *International Herald Tribune*, and spent the rest of that day and half the night rummaging around in the international press reports for periods prior to 1958, focusing on dates nine months prior to Joan's birth. She paid particular attention to articles and by-lines in the *International Herald Tribune* that related to the Caribbean and Martinique. It was late in the evening when she finally struck gold.

From the 274th to the 277th day preceding Joan Chatrier's entry into the world, there'd been big doings in Fort de France, Martinique. A French government munitions expert had traveled from Paris to rendezvous with two revolutionary soldiers who'd island-hopped across the Caribbean to discuss the terms and means of delivery of light arms and ammunition much-needed for their final push to revolutionary victory. These two visitors to Fort de France were treated as celebrities. They'd remained on the island for three days, basking in the success of their mission, and attending to the details on the how and when of the arms drop into the mountains north of Santiago, Cuba.

Martinique's beautiful people, including without a doubt a stunning, nineteen-year-old Mari Roland, had thrown two days of parties . . . dancing and drinking in the streets of Fort de France. Kate collected copies of dated headlines, photos from the Island newspaper, and by-lines with pictures from the *International Herald Tribune*'s Paris edition, which described the occasion and published pictures of two fatigue-clad visitors dancing and cavorting with the most beautiful of the Island's young women, one of whom looked unmistakably familiar.

Kate would be out in California in two days. She'd play with Gordon his favorite game of "What If," and tease him about his pivotal role in putting the biological daughter of Fidel Castro or Che Guevara onto the Supreme Court of the United States. She couldn't say which one. Even Judd needed Mari to answer that question.

* * *